Dear Kiss

Dear Kiss

A Novel of
Love and Life in the Victorian West

Margaret Bagley

E. L. Marker
Salt Lake City

E. L. Marker, an imprint of WiDō Publishing
Salt Lake City, Utah
widopublishing.com

Cover design by Steven Novak
Book design by Marny K. Parkin

ISBN 978-1-947966-32-1

Contents

To MY GRANDPARENTS:
Dora Pauline Hatch Holther, 1869–1955, and Louis Jensen Holther Jr., 1868–1907. *Dear Kiss* is inspired by their letters and by the lives they lived.

Introduction

IT BEGAN WITH PHOTOS OF LOU AND DORA, he in a West Point uniform, she in a classroom photo when she was about sixteen, her serious expression masking a coquettish personality. I had the advantage of knowing Dora, my grandmother, until 1955. She died at eighty-six, paralyzed for years due to a stroke. She had been a widow since 1907, when she was left alone with three children, the youngest, my father, Jack in the story. He was less than two when his father died; he was fascinated by the history his mother related through the years, about the details of their life together. Lou and Dora had been married in 1890. By 1898, they had lost two children to Scarlet Fever.

When I came into possession of their letters, stored for nearly a century with other possessions in our basement, I focused on a small kid purse. Inside was treasure, a handful of ribbon bound letters covering most of their time together from 1883 to 1907. Based on the chronology of the letters, I attempted to craft a narrative. I filled in the blanks, added events, provided some additional characters, and used the words of the letters themselves for the authentic dialogue. A fabric of events surfaced, showing humor, frustration, jealousy, steadfastness, and defeat.

The letters give a distinct view of Ogden at the end of the 19th century and the beginning of the 20th century. They are all authentic. Lou wrote the letter to Dora's mother, the Montana travel directions, the euchre challenge, the faux legal document and the letter to little Darling, as well as others. Lou and Dora kept back and forth exchanges for nearly twenty years.

All my family including Eliza's parents are buried in the Ogden City Cemetery except Jess, my uncle, who is buried elsewhere. I have chosen the names Malan and Hatch because they come from my family.

Frank Elgin, his sister Annie, Nan and Burton French are all fictional characters. The island getaway in the Canyon is real and belonged to my uncle, Jess Holther.

All items mentioned, including the Bo Peep toy and Dora's purse, are in the blue chest, which is now in my bedroom. I imagined the shoes from Marshall Fields. I gave Lou's gold watch, prominent in the story, to my youngest son John, who lives in Park City with his family.

Tillie McGaw and her sister May were school friends of Dora. I have the original letters including the one in the yellow envelope.

References to current events are surprisingly scant but more importantly, the daily pulse of intermountain life, excitement over new business coming to town because of the railroad, parades, celebrations, in all, Ogden pride comes through. Since I lived in Ogden, I recall buildings such as the old Broom Hotel and many other sites, buildings and personages who moved about the downtown area. Many are referenced emphasizing the commercial heartbeat of the community.

Place names and events are as accurate as I required, and since this is a work of fiction, I have altered what served the story. I have also inserted references directly from my grandmother's comments concerning codes of conduct, dress, deportment, customs; even to execution of folk dance patterns for the *Varsouvienne,* performed so many decades before with my grandfather, the familiar haunting tune often used in vintage Western films.

I hope my grandparents would be pleased with my efforts to tell my fictionalized account of their story. Their legacy continues with my children and grandchildren as they hear of those who came before, whose lives, choices, joys and frustrations, made their lives a reality.

Part One
The Euchre Player

Chapter One
Eliza

Ogden, Utah, 1879

A shrill whistle cut through Eliza Jensen's thoughts as a train moved through the rail yards a few miles west of her home. She had just left the warmth of her kitchen and come onto the porch. She rolled down her sleeves, releasing clouds of flour. Shielding her eyes with one hand, she looked north toward Ben Lomond, the majestic mountain peak anchoring the north rim of the Ogden Valley.

An image blurred as she focused on a figure moving toward her on the dusty road, her eleven-year-old son Lou no doubt, returning from his uncle's smithy. She smiled. He embodied all that defined boys of his age; perhaps a bit taller than some, but surely, powdery dust covered him as he scuffed along. Eliza turned her eyes east toward Observatory Peak, rosy in the light. She liked the placement of their modest home on the bench, a ledge formed long ago, part of the shoreline of Lake

Bonneville, an ancient inland sea, the Great Salt Lake being a remnant.

She untied her apron. A loud crack sounded as she flapped it several times, clearing it of flour and bits of dough. She tied it around her waist and re-entered her kitchen. From the window, she could see her energetic son running the last fifty yards, his lungs burning, she imagined, with the effort. His prize would be a hearty lunch and conversation. Eliza always answered his questions about the habits of area birds and animals, as she too found them fascinating.

Lou thumped across the porch and entered the kitchen, emitting the scent of exertion and activity. He held five small rabbits which he had killed and skinned.

"How did you find your uncle, Lou?" Eliza took the game, setting them on a board by the sink.

"Lost the foal from last week but all else is okay."

Eliza nodded toward the sink. "Make sure the scrubbing goes above your wrists."

Lou reached for the large bar of soap. A rough towel lay beside it for drying. They exchanged a comfortable smile between them, substituting for the usual hug.

"There's bread and jam on the table, milk in the cooler, but the stew, thanks to your rabbits, won't be ready 'til supper."

Eliza was a midwife by training. She had been called by the Presidency of The Church of Jesus Christ of Latter-day Saints to travel east to Philadelphia with other women, to gain additional medical training, including surgical skills. This enabled her to attend to emergency needs. Practicing physicians in Ogden welcomed the additional help.

Sometimes leaving in a frenzy, Eliza would don heavy work pants to climb aboard a sturdy wagon, counting on her horse Jackson to carry her to her destination. Caught unawares in winter, she often strode through snow drifts, her skirts frozen to her legs. More than once she attended to her patients in her underclothes, her outer garments drying by the fire.

To deal with schedule uncertainties, Eliza had employed a housekeeper, Delia, to oversee the running of her home in her absence. This allowed her freedom to respond to her patients' needs throughout the Ogden Valley. Delia cooked, looked after Lou, his younger brother Joseph and, though she would never admit it, Eliza herself.

Another whistle, a welcome sound indicating commerce and, in Eliza's mind, notes of opportunity as well as an influx of travelers from the east, even adventurous persons who had been to California or the Northwest. At the stop at Ogden's Union Station, passengers might decide to stay and examine possibilities in the intermountain basin.

Lou's father, Louis Jensen Sr., was thirty-four when he had traveled west with his pregnant, eighteen-year-old wife in 1868 after their marriage in St. Louis. They had made the trek with a handcart company after joining the Church. Lou was born in 1868 soon after they reached the Salt Lake Valley. Subsequently, they decided to move to Ogden where they were welcomed by other church members.

A few years later, after the birth of their youngest son, Joseph, Louis returned twice to his birthplace near Christiana, Norway on missions for the LDS Church. Information had then reached Eliza that her husband had also visited Sweden, where he had married two more women, establishing new families.

On his most recent return home, Louis informed Eliza that he had married an additional wife in the Temple in Manti, to the south of Salt Lake. This information determined her course of action, given not only the information itself, but her understanding of the bounds of intimacy between married couples. At Eliza's insistence, Louis and his newest wife had moved to rooms over his tailor shop nearer the downtown area. He had frequent contact with his sons, and to Eliza's credit, they never seemed to think less of him. In Eliza's mind, however, Louis Sr. received less in the bargain.

After all, Eliza could bake, can and sew with the best of her neighbors; and she had sewn many of her children's clothes, though she preferred her own outer clothing be ready made. Her coats, skirts, and bodices, needed to be serviceable, and she had an eye for style. When meeting with the women's medical group in Salt Lake, Eliza knew the eyes of the other women attending turned when she presented herself. She was striking rather than delicate, her hair flecked with grey, done in a softer style than many of her colleagues who wore tightly

waved hair, a severe center part separating the left side
from the right. Eliza's intense dark eyes signaled intel-
ligence. Her mouth was often pursed in concentration as
she attended lectures, but she was generous in laughter
among family and her closest friends.

Eliza, hearing yet another train whistle, took it as a
signal to put aside more inner thoughts and turn to the
task at hand, that of preparing a delicious stew for herself and her boy.

Chapter Two
Lou

"Where's your pa, Lou?"

An innocent enough question, although yelled rather than asked, the speaker being Ben Coulter, a new boy at the school.

A dusty schoolyard scuffle ensued, resulting in a scraped face for Lou, his blouse now grimy with playground dirt and cinders. Ben loudly complained of a sprained thumb due to the unrelenting hold applied by Lou at the onset of the fight.

The crowd dispersed as Miss Tomlinson came onto the school porch. Experienced enough to know that sorted out issues were better lessons than her seldom used switch could provide, her eyes narrowed as she surveyed the altercation below.

Lou's friends then educated the new boy as they urged him toward the school fence where his instruction continued. Lou's father, Louis Jensen Sr., lived with his second wife close to the downtown area. Mrs. Jensen lived with their schoolmate, Lou, his younger brother, Joseph, and a housekeeper. No further details were provided, except that many of the schoolchildren's younger brothers and sisters had been delivered by mid-wife Jensen.

The boys suggested Ben address future questions to his parents, who were Mormon converts themselves.

ᴑ⸺

As Lou passed his twelfth birthday, he hated having some-one stay with him when his mother was away, though Eliza now had a hired man for heavy chores and care of her horses. He had taught Lou how to play Euchre, and Lou's skill at the game enhanced his standing with many of his classmates.

As the eldest son, Lou acquired special privileges and more leeway for activities outside Ogden Central School where he was a student. Studies, as fall arrived, carved time away from home, card playing and exploring the foothills with his friends.

Though he wanted desperately to have a horse of his own, his mother made the case that her practice depended on the reliability and availability of her own horses. Lou awaited future opportunities for pleading his own need. In particular, Lou sought to prove to his mother that he was trustworthy and could become adept in handling her horse and buggy.

Lou had freedom to question and venture out, with-out undue parental constraints concerning what he read or studied, or which activities he pursued, at school or in the downtown community. He followed whatever drew his interest. His father's tailor shop was near town and Lou often stopped in to say hello.

When not in school, Lou spent time gathering information. He hung around the handsome courthouse soaking up conversation, peppered with legal terms and newspaper jargon as the reporters sought details on the latest row near the railroad depot, or latest political upset. For Lou, this felt like the very heartbeat of the city. He deftly weaved his way around the courthouse halls, memorizing locations of various offices of the court and county.

His inner conversation involved briefs, torts, and summary judgments, a particular favorite, all combined in a made-up running dialog in his head. Happily, he inhaled the smell of tobacco, ink, newsprint, sweat and leather, the masculine essence of the building.

Two of the lawyers, young Handy and Bert Meeker, took time to explain terms to him. Soon he inadvertently peppered his conversation, most of it to himself, with what was going on this week in which judge's chambers, and which probate revelations would have caused raised eyebrows. Lou found even the dry examination of abstracts in real property, necessary for land transfers, interested him. The very word "litigation" caused him to move quickly to master facts concerning amicus briefs, his newly acquired favorite.

Though law might be seen as a path for Lou, the commercial hubbub seemed more accessible than more academic endeavors. Business chatter and gossip about a store opening made use of lessons being learned from his first employer, David Kay, a successful wholesale grocer offering produce and more, including domestic and imported fruit, and even an extensive seed inventory.

The clamor and vitality of Ogden drew him. As time passed, most of the people who knew him tagged Lou a bright young man.

Lou had already decided against medicine as a career. He saw that the routine of his mother's life went beyond what he envisioned for himself and a future family. The clamor and vitality of town was what attracted him. He was a voracious reader and agile in retrieving discarded newspapers and advertisements as well as political information bills as they fell from the hands of passersby. This kept him abreast of current happenings even beyond more traditional means.

His reading interests broadened and, as he made more friends at school, Lou saw it necessary to acquire the habit and adroitness of passing notes in class to maintain social interaction. More recently he sought to hone phrases and clever salutations, which he believed showed greater sophistication.

After he met Dora Pauline Barlow of Mound Fort, he worked especially hard to perfect his declarations. Since she lived some miles to the north, the approaching need for access to the household buggy became his primary focus in order to properly court her.

Chapter Three
Dora

The letter was addressed with Lou's customary flourishes to Miss Dora Barlow, Ogden City. The date was February 24, 1882. Inside was a note to be delivered to the principal of Ogden Central School, Prof. Talbot Morris. The message was brief: *Dear Sir, Kindly deliver to Miss Dora Barlow all my goods and chattels lately left behind at my unseemly exit from school, sometime hence. Yours truly, I remain, Louis Jensen Jr.* Lou was fourteen.

As Dora read this latest communication from Lou, she felt party to yet another of his escapades. To others, this message might seem the most ordinary request, surely a favor ably carried out by Bill Baker, or even Joe, his brother. But no, she was given an almost conspiratorial assignment and, in the bargain, identified as partner. She chuckled as she tapped the edge of the note against her smiling lips.

Socially Dora had learned to conduct herself properly, returning calls with her mother. She sat patiently in the parlors of her mother's friends as they exchanged gossip, recipes and personal medical advice that Dora thought better shared in private. Being somewhat squeamish, she was uninterested in womanly physical functions which would concern her more in the future.

Dora often cringed at the whining comments of Cora Hansen who once again recounted her latest childbirth and nursing challenges. For now, Dora preferred the outward signs of inner womanhood, following the requirements laid down by her parents, seeking only their approval; or more often, her mother's "That's nice, dear," followed by a double pat on Dora's folded hands.

At times, Dora felt that she actually glowed in her mother's domestic reflection. She had perfected the art of a well-written thank you note, never straying from proper phrases, though her mother cautioned her against the use of wavy lines under words she wished to highlight such as "too lovely" or "simply delicious." Dora kept her scalloped edged cards in a tissue lined box to guard against smudges or creases.

Dora's eyes rested on her mother's benign smile as she presided over the evening meal. Inevitably, Dora's health, or her father's perception of it, would be highlighted. Dora was aware that some of the pallor he commented on was due to the dim overhead light under which they dined. Her father's rugged and weather worn face at the opposite end of the table contrasted sharply with his womenfolk, whose bonnets and gloves protected their skin. Still, his directive intoned that she should "partake of God's bounteous provision of fresh air and sunshine, available to all of us." She heard it with regularity. Behind his back, Dora watched her brother Viv as he silently mouthed the oft repeated edict to tease her.

Dora refrained from visibly reacting to her mother's acquiescence regarding her health. Pinching Dora's cheeks to bring up the color was, in the end, not a suitable solution. A need to be the center of attention was not part of Dora's personality, at least when the attention came from her parents.

In the privacy of the room the girls shared, Dora unburdened herself. "What could they know of my perceptions and dreams, of my interactions with friends? They're old, Nannie. We have to accept that. They will never change. But, of course, we will still love them and act in an obedient manner."

"You mean like when our cousin came up with a way to make your cheeks rosy?" Nannie said.

Dora's sister Nancy, called Nannie from infancy, could be persuaded by Dora to take on the outside chores, which Dora disliked; although she never tired of the endless round of kneading, scrubbing and boiling, to say nothing of work at the dining table after the meal, along with mending and learning the sewing techniques necessary to produce handwork to lay away for her future home. Each finished item was stored in a simple maple chest at the foot of her mother's bed.

Even when Dora showed Nannie the treasure of snowy linens laid inside by her mother and grandmother and which would be hers one day, Nannie only shrugged her shoulders, which infuriated Dora. "Nannie, you are so ungrateful for all mother and I do to have a lovely home. How are you ever going to learn how to make a good nest, if you don't learn now from our mother?"

"You make it sound like we are of the bird family." Nannie read widely and was especially interested in birds. This further irritated Dora, but she let the comment go unanswered.

Dora's cousin, Kit Budge from Logan, had shared her own discovery copied from her friend Ovedia Jex. The girls soon found a way to use this method right in the Barlow dining room. On one of Kit's visits, the girls moved the sideboard out from the wall enough to allow them to crouch behind it. Close to the floor, Kit scraped a small powdery amount of pigment from the wallpaper. The girls agreed the powder was an imaginative way to augment nature's bloom.

The cranberry red paper, had anyone looked, would have revealed in the subsequent months, multiple light patches on the paper near the floor. Dora used a fluff of cotton wool to apply a judicious amount of the substance to her cheeks. The powder was kept in her room on a discarded chipped saucer. Dora gauged the effect of the faint smudge in the mirror above the tall dresser she shared with Nannie. The mirror hung above their bureau at an inconvenient height for the girls, since their father had thought this an effective restraint against too much primping.

Standing on tiptoe, Dora could see that her formerly pale cheeks soon glowed with a subtle rose hue. She carefully blended in the color with a soft cloth, mixing in a small amount of orange blossom powder, a cosmetic her mother allowed along with Florida Water. Dora had convinced her mother that her restored healthy appearance was due to the iron tonic which her father had suggested.

Dora had overheard her parents discussing Lou's mother, Mrs. Jensen, and her brusque manner. She was relieved when she heard her mother's evaluation of a well-ordered life, allowing for domestic as well as professional commitments, although Dora's mother chuckled at the knowledge that Eliza Jensen had help in her home.

Dora mulled over these overheard observations concerning Lou's parents. She saw them as mild. The most objectionable observation seemed to be her mother's opinions about Mr. Jensen no longer living in the home, but with his second wife elsewhere.

One evening after dinner, Dora strained to catch her parents' comments. "You should be concerned about Dora's future, as her father. Concerned about her future in-laws, in fact. I don't mind that Eliza Jensen sees to the medical needs of the community, though we have never called on her."

"Now, my dear," Dora caught the mild voice of her father for a brief beginning comment.

"Let me finish. She runs a home for bad girls, I have heard that too, or girls in trouble, Minnie Baker told me. And she talks about women's rights and such, I mean beyond voting. And she travels alone, all the way to Chicago!"

Dora almost doubled up at this outburst. Dear Lou, lovely boy that he was, had a mother who traveled alone! Dora only hoped that as she took her place as Lou's wife someday, he would trust her to travel alone, at least to Salt Lake on the Bamberger train to visit relatives. All in all, this would not make a difference in their "romance". Dora thrilled to the word he used routinely to convey the progression of their relationship. Sure that her parents were totally unaware of the frequency of their correspondence, she couldn't imagine giving up this essential daily link to him.

Dora, on an afternoon call with her mother, heard Polly Hatch say it was rumored that Mrs. Jensen was a staunch supporter of "women's rights" and had corresponded with like-minded ladies in Chicago and Boston and, more recently, in the intermountain region.

Dora later learned from Lou that Eliza was a fine seamstress making most, though not all, of her family's clothes. Her store-bought bodices were of the latest cut, in Dora's estimation. An opinion formed one afternoon in town as Dora and a friend saw Mrs. Jensen cross Washington Avenue. Dora was surprised to hear Lou evaluate her cooking. He said her recipes were more unusual than local substantial fare. His mother had sampled many dishes at friends' homes while living for a time in Philadelphia. Lou declined some of her dishes containing cumin and oregano and would not eat anchovies. Dora imagined that at some future date, she herself would partake of a meal at the Jensen home.

Chapter Four
Lou

On the letterhead from Harris Bros. Shipping, featuring the tri-arched front on the store and a horse and wagon passing, Dora read a short apology: *Dora, I cannot see you until Wednesday! I go to Salt Lake and can't get out of it. Yours, Lou, sorry to disappoint, please excuse.*

As she held the paper in her hand, Dora smiled knowing that the dashed off note was not that at all but a carefully worded message to her. She loved the comment, "sorry to disappoint, please excuse." My, but Lou did favor what he had overheard or read; and now and then was inventive himself in the turn of a phrase, one that would draw her admiration. No worry about her interest in him. It had been sealed completely in her mind and his as well. They knew they would go on and on, for time and all eternity, even if Lou wasn't the most devout Mormon youth and didn't seem to take all the teachings to heart.

Reflecting on her friend Tillie's notes and opinions further confirmed the unassailable truth that their friends and family expected them to marry. Still, a comment of Tillie's: "Have you met Lou's mother? I don't think she's in your mother's mold at all" had given Dora pause.

Dora was surprised to receive by mail a short note from Lou's mother. At first, she thought Lou wrote it for a tease, but he denied it and laughed when she showed it to him. It began, *To Miss Dora Barlow from Mrs. Louis Jensen Sr., Please bear in mind young lady that my son is permitted to go to but one dance and one theatre each week hereafter, yours, respectfully, Mrs. Louis Jensen.*

"Could Joe have written it?" Dora asked Lou at school the next day.

He responded, "Well, it's not the way she would normally write. She just might have dashed it off in a fit of pique, because I am seeing only you and not even thinking of any of the other girls my age."

Lou winked. "My mother has not been subtle about her opinions. She said just the other day, 'What is wrong with the Pingrees and the Cardens? The Harris girls are both very accomplished.' Of course, I just stared at the wall or something, without saying a word."

Dora smiled at Lou's imitation of his mother's voice saying the words.

A moment later, Lou said, "We probably should ignore this for the time being. You just don't know, Dora, how hard she works. And in the future, she will come to depend on me as she gets older and as I mature."

Dora was not happy at the somber tone, but she tried to see his reasoning.

A few days after receiving the note from Lou's mother came a more welcome arrival. Dora received the type of message she most enjoyed reading: *Dora, A crowd of us is going out in the large bobsleigh this eve and I should be pleased to have your company. So, if you choose to go, we will call at or about 7 o'clock, Your Lou.*

Her Lou. The note inviting her to a favorite activity, one that allowed them to be close in the cold winter air, covered with warm rugs and fleeces, hurling through the snow, bumping over the fields and screaming with delight with their friends. Nothing suited Dora more. Since this was certainly not a dance or a matinee, Mrs. Jensen's objections were not transgressed.

A few weeks later, came the invitation to a sewing bee. Lizzie Croft wrote to Dora: *I should like very much to have you there. We are going to have such fun and all of the girls are supposed to fetch their fellows so you know what to do. Now don't be bashful in asking Lou to come. Try and come down at 7:30 if possible, Yours truly, Lizzie.*

Dora was delighted to be known with Lou as a couple as they negotiated the social and school activity whirl so much to her liking. Added to this was the fact that her parents had told her they were more than happy at the future marriage. There was even talk of the wedding itself, where it was to take place, whom would officiate.

Dora, Lizzie, Tillie and May spent no more time than was normal discussing all things matrimonial, having a somewhat incomplete appreciation of the full scope of housewifely duties. All of them, including Nannie, Dora's sister, were pressed into service minding babies, polishing furniture, peeling apples for pies in their respective homes as part of weekly routine.

Because of some of the hardship lessons of older family members, the girls were shielded from some of the harsher realities of life. The mysteries of the sickroom and infrequent visits of a wayward cousin of the Barlows, in particular, was hushed up. Dora's father shielded his family from anything coarse or vulgar and, over the heads of the children at the dinner table, communicated in an effective way with his wife.

Chapter Five
Love Notes

As Dora unfolded the current letter, she saw it was clearly dashed off. Lou's writing was not as ornate as usual, a spontaneous and urgent message he wanted to transfer to her, perhaps on a whim, with just a hint of naughtiness; the not so subtle message on the envelope, in very small script: *With such declamations as are herein contained, it would be unwise to carry this around in the bosom of your jersey like you generally do, your Lou.*

Inside, the swirls of Lou's penmanship knew no bounds and it matched the content of the message. The words fairly spun across the page.

Dora, kindly excuse me until seven-thirty this evening. Am scheduled to preach in the fourth ward, Ha! Ha! Ha! your devoted admirer, Lou. Remember eve of 3/12/96?

Their progression had moved with very few missteps from the time they were first acquainted in school to participating in church and other social activities. Therefore, each time they came together, and every written communication which passed between them, forged additional links in the tender chain which bound them.

Dora often looked at a photograph taken of the couple in a Sunday school grouping. The photographer, Mr. Pasevitch, insisted on placing the boys on the back row because of their height. Dora was not pleased with her facial expression but, since Lou teased her about it in a fun-felt way, she couldn't complain. All students were instructed to look straight ahead, but the sitting ended when all erupted in laughter as the group chased the photographer's cat around the room to prevent it from escaping down the stairs.

Dora held to a high standard of decorum, but in the following letter, she read the true evidence of their romantic path.

May twenty-first, 1887: *My Darling Dora, Am in receipt of a somewhat unwelcome denial of the possibility of a "date" for a ride in the company of "my ideal" but as you have made an appointment and consider mine secondary, I shall willingly comply with your request. It pains me Dora to hear you speak of nervousness, indeed my love, I wish to God I had more control of myself. If such was the case, I think we would be, at least you, would be happy, but since an all wise Creator has seen fit to curse me as "Passion's Slave," so mote it be. Dora, you do not realize how hard I struggle to overcome this inordinate passion but it all seems in vain. I hope that in the future, by some almost super human effort, I may be able to present myself to you as an honorable and upright youth of God. Dora,*

I have a conscience and my heart is good but my resolutions are weak. It's hard to cast this spell off when bound by the powers of the devil. Does this make me vile and debased in your eyes, my darling? Your presence is always before me and now and then you say I love you out loud and that buoys me up. I had the blues last week so bad, I don't know scarcely how to stand it. I feel like I'm not like other boys my age. I've been brought up to have sensitive feelings, but I still have melancholy times. I might say there is too much "sex" about me, but I always was a black sheep and born to worry. I'll not transport my feelings to you, but trouble told makes it much lighter. Tonight the theatre was a possibility but though nothing would give me more pleasure, I have my Sunday school lesson to prepare tonight and won't be through before seven thirty at the earliest and then to get the buggy and get to you—you see it would be too late but if you could manage to come over to town (couldn't Viv bring you?) then I should be delighted if this comes to pass. Dora, as sure as there is a God in heaven, I love you better than any other creature He ever created. In case you come, where shall I call for you, if I can get our buggy, Tillie might get a note to me but of course if I receive no word, I shall consider you cannot go, all of which is optional. Don't think me a fool for writing this way and at such length but it is exactly as I felt and I wrote it and now feel better, if I see you today, I know all shall be okay, Truly, your ardent and devoted admirer and lover, L. Don't write such cold notes.

Dora's hand shook as she opened her scalloped notepaper to dash as quickly as possible a return note to Lou.

Her pencil flew as she sped to get the words out to her boy. Though paragraph form was followed, she rubbed out and started words over several times trying to get to Lou this way, though she longed to rush into his arms.

Same date: *My dearest one, I cannot go tonight because ma expects me to go to town and I have promised to mind some neighbor children 'til then, and I can't go back on my promise. Lou, you do not know how pleased I would be if you would spend the eve with me after your class. Could you get here? Ma and pa will be at Clawson's, only Viv will be here studying. Hoping this letter will not get cold before you get it, I remain, devotedly, Dora.*

The "D" was executed with a flourish but in no way equaled what Lou might have produced. Underlined with a subtle wave were the words am and very, words in themselves of no particular weight at all but in the hands, mind and receiving eyes of Lou, they were steamy with intent.

Chapter Six
A Trusted Courier, and One Not to be Ignored

When Dora was sixteen, she received her teaching certificate awarded by Weber County Superintendent of Schools, Utah Territory. She passed the examination with an above average grade, certified as having good moral character and an aptness for teaching. Her initial assignment was for one year.

A note from Lou, delivered by Tillie, included this phrase: *Formerly my best girl, now a woman and equipped to earn her daily bread, but please let me be the one to assume that pleasant burden, L.*

When they were together that afternoon, and she showed him the document, he took a moment to look it over carefully. As he did so, Dora stood, drawing herself up to her full five feet five-and one-half inches, and, as she cast a sideways glance in the hallway mirror, raised her shoulders and squared them for effect.

She bristled only a bit as Lou chided her for a low mark in physiology. Still, she knew he was proud of this goal reached. In their future, this meant she was better prepared than most women to charge and instruct their own children as they entered the school system. For her part, Dora found she indeed had an aptitude for explaining concepts in a simple way. More importantly, not appearing overbearing and bossy the way some of her friends who had achieved the certificate with her did. She kept the treasured paper in an envelope so that if needed, it would be unwrinkled and presentable. She thought she just might use it to apply for a teaching position someday.

Received from Tillie, the couple's courier, in an envelope addressed in swirled script with thickened letters to begin each word, the formality hinted, but did not reveal, the reason for the communication.

Inside the envelope, the note began, *Ogden 4/24/87. Miss Barlow, providing you have made no arrangements for tomorrow evening, I should be delighted to have the pleasure of your company. An early answer will oblige, Lou.* The message was perfectly placed, paced and indented on the heavy white stock. Knowing Lou, Dora could imagine that on his desk were sheets of paper covered with practice letters incorporating the scrolls necessary for the elegant show he wanted.

From the beginning of the year and into the spring, the letters had flown between them. Tillie and her sister May were the usual couriers. However, Tillie of late, focused on her poor health, admitted to a frequent need to miss school. She complained to Dora that she didn't visit her often enough and, without subtlety, referred to other friends who found the time to stop by after school. Dora knew her friend had her eyes on Joe, Lou's younger brother. She also was aware that Joe's feelings were not as deep as Tillie might have wanted. Joe would have been very uncomfortable to see the string of "x o x o x o" which Tillie explicitly sent to him at the end of her notes to Dora.

One afternoon when Dora did find time to stop by, Tillie exclaimed, "Dora, my concern knows no bounds, and I have worried myself sick that you are less healthy than I. This really can't be borne!"

In Dora's opinion, the countless notes, filled as they were with hyperbole, were a form of entertainment as well as a conduit for gossip; and, at times, thinking out loud about how she, Tillie, was going to end up with the boy of her dreams. One letter was delivered enclosed in a yellow envelope. At the bottom left hand corner, Tillie had, in tiny script, explained she had used yellow because she was jealous. Dora had told Tillie in no uncertain terms she might as well target Joe, since it was out of the question that Lou would ever be swayed by her extravagant phrases. The next best choice was Joe; and to bolster Tillie's hope somewhat, Dora resorted to the old cliché that, "still waters run deep." Tillie rolled her eyes.

Thursday, Dora Darling, over a week has passed without my receiving a letter from you. I hope illness isn't the cause. Pray write quickly or I shall be inclined to think you an idle girl. I hope no other girl confidant is undermining

*your affections so that you're confiding all about Lou.
Think, dear girl, of the notes I have carried to him on
your behalf. Now write a long letter to me as speedily as
your dainty fingers can produce. I asked May if she had
seen you and she said no. I had the doctor Saturday. Rose
came over yesterday to keep me company and stayed all
afternoon. Even Carrie Baker, you know her brother Bill,
dropped in. Now enough scolding. Love to Joe if you see
him, Tillie.*

At times, Lou would send a somewhat formal invitation to an activity, written on letterhead, usually David
Kay's, where Lou worked at the time. One unique offering showed his humor if not his industriousness.

*Office of Louis Jensen Wholesale and Retail White-
washer. Jobs taken by the piece or by the day, Ogden,
April 2, 1887. Parties desiring fancy work in this line executed, would do well to consult me personally. Barns and
parlors a specialty. L. J. Jensen Jr.*

*Dora, this evening The Recherche Ball occurs. Do you
wish to go? Will call however, and if you do not wish to go,
alright. Please excuse me having to use a letterhead. It is
all the paper I have in my desk. Yours, Lou.*

As the months rolled by, Dora became even more used
to his unconventional invitations and his unabashed
means of calling attention to what he was doing, catching her eye on a daily basis as if any other would-be
suitor could possibly compete for her attention. All that
Lou was and experienced, he sought to share with her. A
camping excursion with friends was one more reason to

show his manly interests yet without façade, revealing his self-effacing approach to life.

From Swan Creek mid-summer: *Dear Dora, we are now about to start for home on the edge of Bear Lake. This is the finest sheet of water I ever saw. It is fresh water eight miles by twenty I think and as clear as crystal and deep as sheol. We have a boat and skein at our disposal, but we cannot work the sail and the fish won't bite our fly hook. We can see thousands of them in great schools, but we haven't enticed any to bite. We killed some ducks, but they were "fishy," and we let 'em alone. We had a royal bear scare Saturday night. I know I lost the best ten years of my life through fright but it's all right now. We had no bear steak nor did they feast on us. We are within a block or so of Idaho and over 100 miles from home. I never have had a better time in my life than I am having now. We will reach Ogden on the 11th if we have good luck. We have broken our wagon and lost our team but think we will be all right now. Constantly yours, Lou.*

Dora visualized, as best she could, how, what started out as a weekend excursion, turned into what, for her, would have been nothing short of harrowing. How quickly he bounced back nonetheless for the arduous journey home, which he detailed only to a degree. Their communication routine resumed with, for the most part, gentle teasing and declarations of fidelity. At times Dora wearied of Lou's more flowery recitations of "How far I have stumbled in incurring your wrath" when apologizing over some slight.

Their elders would have been shocked at the informality of their address, B. L. D. meaning beloved Dora, as he began a note: *We have seats for this evening so be sure you are ready, chippy, 7:45 sharp. It is useless to ask you to send the boy back with an answer for you don't know that much, do you? I had to send the boy back for an answer last time because you did not have enough sense to reply yes or no, whether or not you could go out or not. A gentle rebuke, I adore you, goodbye prec. (precious), L.*

A more recent issue arose involving a running joke between them about Lou not giving Dora time enough to decide what she would wear to an event; in this case, the Recherche Ball. The note, so typical of Lou, reaffirmed that of course they would go together. Dora's dress had three weeks ago been finished, her mother making over one of her own gowns worn years before and made of plum velvet. She thought it had more drama than what her two closet friends had chosen.

Chapter Seven
Courting and Conflict

Challenge! By these presents I send greeting to Miss Dora Barlow. You are hereby challenged to meet me, in friendly contest, at a game of Euchre for the ice cream or tooth picks, your choice and place, mine of trumps, yours truly, L. J. Jensen, the Euchre player, Ogden, September sixth 1888.

The short document was in green type and spaced neatly on a half sheet. Lou had given the messenger twenty cents to deliver it. Dora never tired of the unique invitations from Lou. In the case of the Euchre challenge, travel south from Mound Fort was denied, due to a tree at the Barlow home falling near their front porch. Dora's mother, in a state, argued that Dora had to be at home to help establish calm. To Dora it seemed a tepid request; but the travel, and therefore the game, was postponed.

One afternoon Lou and Dora took Eliza's wagon, pulled by the work horse she had allowed the couple to use. An easy drive brought them to the foothills just below Observatory Peak. Dora was relieved to end the bumpy ride and to further distance themselves from their elders. The couple had planned the afternoon in the canyon complete with food and refreshment, to allow them time to talk privately about their future. The approaching separation in the fall was uppermost in their minds. Lou assumed their perspectives would differ somewhat.

Lou's mother Eliza had told him about an inquiry she had made regarding the process for applying to the military academy at West Point. Within a few weeks, without input from Lou, she made all arrangements for him to take the written examination. The final physical and in person interview would occur when he reached West Point.

Not long afterward, Lou shared with Dora his excitement about his appointment to the United States Military Academy as, he stated, "any able-bodied youth would be." He as yet had no realistic view of exactly what would be required academically. He knew no one with whom he could correspond, who could reassure him it would be within his capabilities.

Dora stated, "What sense does it make after your family brought you, at least, forgive me if I'm being indelicate, in your mother's body, across the plains and now it's no good to go to school here? Why West Point? You're not interested in the Army, never even talked about it."

Dora knew that Lou's mother had come into the Salt Lake Valley in 1868. Dora had shared with Lou her romantic imaginings, helped along by a photo he had shown her of his mother, twenty years younger. Eliza sat in a photographer's chair, a new mother holding a scrawny Lou, naked on her lap, her hair loose about her shoulders, her face, not serene but triumphant.

This was the woman Dora visualized striding into the valley with her handcart. Her cheeks would have been bronzed, her hands calloused, her feet shod in high sturdy boots, battered from the journey. Lou's mother had often told him about how sore her heels were for weeks after her arrival. Adding drama was the fact that Eliza was nearly nine months pregnant and delivered within two weeks of the company's arrival.

As Dora imagined it, the wind would have been blowing as Eliza's skirts billowed about her legs. Lou's father would have been behind her; though what Dora based this on was obscure, as she tried to imagine him vigorous and strapping like Lou. Dora had seen Louis Jensen Sr. only a few times.

The journey across the plains was adventure for some, an uneventful crossing for a few, and a harrowing experience for others. In the comfort of the Barlow home, many recollections and journal accounts were shared. The uncertainty would have undone Dora. Particularly riveting was a friend's description of a ten-year-old boy drowned in a rush of water as they crossed what they thought was a benign creek. The current carried the boy away downstream, wedging him in rocks and brush while his mother and company watched, helpless to reach him.

Lou squinted as he stood above Dora on a ledge. His gaze westward took in the valley, the horizon only a shimmering blur. The couple had climbed a short distance from where they stopped the wagon. He urged Dora wordlessly to take his hand. She shook her head and sat down on the prickly grass.

"Not every boy who goes to West Point is looking to be an Army man, Pol."

"Don't talk to me like I'm a child, Lou."

"Well, you've got a certificate." Lou smiled as he cradled her hands in his. Dora gently swatted him on his chest as he jumped down to her level. "You know it won't be that long. Ma would bring you back to see me, I'll bet." Lou spoke confidently and reassuringly, surprised at Dora's vigorous return.

"I can't imagine in any circumstance that happening at all." She turned away from him.

He knew the tears would follow. He saw her squint. But she continued with the vigor he had seen before when she put forth an opinion different from his.

"Tell me what you would study there, that you couldn't study here, down at Salt Lake. You could even be a doctor, Lou."

"I don't want to be a doctor! I just like running the store and fishing and hunting and knowing what's going on in town and at the Elks." Lou pressed on, "I'll go back, see New York, Philadelphia, maybe Boston." Warming to his message, he placed his hands on Dora's shoulders with a light touch. "Then I'll go to school for a year and get a start on engineering maybe, and then . . ."

"And then, I would do what? Stay at Mound Fort with ma, and Nannie is going to marry first, I just know it!"

"Let her! Think of it, getting ready for our wedding, planning where we're going to live." He sought to draw her closer, but she stiffened.

"You'll probably want to move in with your mother; and, Lou, she stares icicles at me sometimes."

Lou couldn't deny this perception. "No sir, not if I have to build a place myself!" He pulled Dora close, their bodies warm against each other. The sun's heat intensified the smell of cotton and, for Lou, the unmistakable scent of lavender.

Lou had set their fruit juice in a canteen to cool it in the river. He wedged the container between rocks so the current wouldn't jar it loose. They admired the colors now starting to turn as if on cue, even as their sight was mostly for each other alone.

They waded briefly in the running stream but experienced such paralyzing chill about their ankles, they quickly gained the bank and wrapped their legs in the wool blanket, their feet touching in its folds until they warmed.

The day was near perfect. The swish of water, the intoxicating sweet, spicy smell of the canyon in their nostrils, a combination of rocks and soil; and wet willows as they scraped along the banks, a certain leaf, sage perhaps, which emitted the scent. It was as captivating as was the roaring current in their ears as it foamed along the bank. The couple would have to start back to Lou's house so that he could see Dora safely home. They wrapped the blanket more tightly around each other, delaying the return home. Lou imagined lying next to Dora wrapped as they were, if only for a few moments.

"Lou, I can't bear to have you leave me and go back East. You'll never come back! It's so unfair."

"We can write, love."

"Write!" Dora bolted upright, bracing her weight on one arm and breaking the hold Lou sought to secure. "We have written thousands of miles of words. We have talked about everything even married couples talk about, but I want to be close to you, like you said."

Lou squirmed a bit, not sure his words had the effect he intended. He wasn't sure they rang true to himself either. "Now, my darling, we will discover the best way." He placed a finger across her lips and hoped his kiss would still her anxiety.

Instead, she broke free and gathered their blankets. With Lou's help, they broke camp, such as it was.

Lou felt morose as he took the reins. As they plodded along down the gentle incline, he judged that he had joked too much and not given the discussion the seriousness it deserved. Dora had chosen to sit close to him. He was intoxicated by the smell of her warm skin. He longed to have her rest her head on his shoulder and dare to rest her hand on his arm.

To mar the afternoon, Lou saw his mother standing near the barn. She met them as they returned to the rear of the property. Lou had intended to transfer to the buggy so he could drive Dora home. Though the afternoon had turned cool and a brisk wind whipped the poplar trees, Lou's mother stood, arms folded, her shawl barely covering her shoulders.

Her voice grated in the air. "Dora, don't you think the opportunity for my boy to educate himself at West Point is a worthwhile goal?"

Lou saw the color rise in Dora's cheeks. If his mother only knew of the intimacy the couple enjoyed, she might decide that putting off their marriage might be unwise.

Chapter Eight
Marking Time

The letter from Lou arrived by regular post. Jane Dinah Barlow recognized the writing. She settled herself on the settee to read it. Her husband's name had been omitted from the envelope. Dora had told Lou that her father had lost most of his sight.

A slight smile played across her face as she read.

Dear Mrs. Barlow, Kindly excuse me from intruding upon your time for a few moments for I feel that if acting honorable toward you, I must unburden to you my thoughts and feelings. I know it is not right to engage the attention of Dora for any length of time as I have without having in view, a terminus, and I know it would be dishonorable in me to contract any alliance with her without your knowledge, permission and approval.

During the past year I have found in Dora everything I would consider praiseworthy for her age. I know she is pure and virtuous which is to be prized above all things. Of course, I am too young to enter into the married state but consider that you are due the respect, of letting you know what my intentions are.

Now Mrs. Barlow, if you have any objections to my calling on her, knowing what my intentions are, or if you do not consider me worthy of her, I hope you will let me know when I call Sunday, as I shall then expect from you a statement as to whether I shall consider myself a rejected or accepted suiter, whether to continue my visits or discontinue them. It might not be a bad idea to ask Dora about what her feelings are in regard to the matter as it might enable you to arrive at a conclusion.

Please remember that between us this is to remain a secret as many a slip occurs between the cup and the lips and many other obvious reasons for secrecy. I am unable, of course to lecture you on this subject as you are an experienced individual in living, but I have a vague conception of its beauties and its disasters.

Trusting that we may understand each other and that you will have formed an opinion ere Sunday, I remain respectfully, Louis Jensen Jr.

Jane Dinah let the papers rest in her lap. She smiled as she called out, "Oliver." Her husband, who was in the next room, slowly made his way to the chair beside his wife.

∽

Eliza made arrangements for Lou to go East early. She wanted to provide him a chance to tour some of the

Eastern cities so that he wouldn't feel like such a Westerner compared to her friend's son.

Lou was given to speaking well. With his ramrod stature, ash blond hair and green eyes, he was a son to be proud of. Eliza loved Joseph, her youngest son, of course, but Lou was full of promise and ability. So unlike his father or anyone in her family. His facial features were like hers; and she held this pride to her heart, the Nordic height and bearing, his alone. Her former husband was several inches shorter and wobbled as he walked. The sight of Lou striding ahead of her was not her only seed of vanity, but it was a substantial one.

She made sure, as he left, that his belongings were first rate. This included respectable luggage, with a case not unlike those carried by the city's lawyers for books and newspapers.

She cautioned her son, saying, "It is all right to carry a folded paper under your arm when walking down Washington Avenue; but when traveling, it is important to keep track of your things. You should have at the ready ticket and traveling papers. Money should be in a vest pocket and additional cash in a special pocket inside your jacket. I've designed it myself."

Eliza bestowed a self-satisfied smile on her handsome son. After correspondence with her friends, especially one who lived in Boston, she felt sure Lou would present himself as a well-turned-out young man.

～

Mid-summer, Lou left from the Ogden Union Station. He waved exuberantly, his infectious grin bestowed on his enthusiastic farewell party. Dora, part of the adoring crowd, became separated from Lou, who stood with his mother on the platform. The crowd moved as a single entity, and she was drawn farther away still, unable to make eye contact with him. Enveloped in the boisterous group wishing her boy fair travels, Dora stood on tiptoe not to fade completely from his view.

She had worn a burgundy jacket trimmed with a thin border of fur, though it was far from autumn. On such a warm day she would have snatched a serviceable fan from the woman standing next to her, to cool her own face. Of course, that would have defeated the autumnal vision she sought. But Lou was oblivious. Fifteen minutes before, he had hugged her briefly, indeed lifted her off the ground, but as Eliza's eyes flamed, Lou released her. His pledge to write often was wooden.

Dora thought of the many ice cream socials and activities she would attend without her escort. She was always welcome to go with Joe's family, as the couple needed someone to mind their babies, blessed with two barely eleven months apart. Nannie, as Dora predicted, married before Dora and was pregnant, proudly showing her condition. She had told Dora that she was in need of constant companionship since her husband, Edgar, was selling mining equipment and traveling constantly.

As Dora lay across her bed reading to Nannie, she shared how she longed for Lou.

One evening after dinner, Nannie complained to Dora of a sick headache. "I think I'll just go upstairs for a little while. Why don't you write out a note to Lou, just a note, mind you. I know you haven't heard from him."

Dora regretted having shared this news, but then her temper flared at Nannie's additional nudge: "Why don't you call Mrs. Jensen, Dora. She won't bite."

"That's just a ridiculous idea, Nannie. I would be absolutely shamed for her to find out about our broken chain of correspondence." Then at a reduced intensity, "Are you sure you don't want me to come up and read to you? I don't mind, really." Dora fingered the frayed sofa cushion, hoping to stay downstairs longer and make good her own resolve to pen the letter. She did value her sister's counsel, knowing that in the future such an opportunity to be girls together sharing a room would be only a treasured memory.

"Dora, my sick headache will go away better in the dark with a cold cloth over my eyes. Don't come up until you are ready to go to bed. Maybe some cold tea would be nice, it never keeps me awake like ma says."

Dora felt chastised by Nannie. She alone would decide when to write. But as she began a note, she gathered speed, rushing to tell him, not that she missed him already, but how busy she was. Lou mustn't think she just sat on her hands waiting for him.

She had planned to respond only after Lou's first letter, when it came. Perhaps writing a few lines each day as newsy items to keep his attention and connecting to home would be an effective strategy. She sat at a small writing table, the ticking clock emphasizing the escaping hours. Her parents were out for the evening. It was nearly time for her to fix tea for her sister. She would pour a cup of milk for herself and take two pieces of gingerbread to share.

"Dora, maybe you could come up now. I'm lonely," Nannie called.

Folding the note on which she had written, Dear Lou, followed by only three sentences, Dora rushed to her duty.

Chapter Nine
Letters across the Plains

My Darling, Why the cause of such distress? My gosh child, I am almost famished to hear from you, almost three weeks have passed since I left home and you write about how miserable you are.

Dora, skimming ahead, could see words underlined for emphasis.

I can't imagine how many I've written, even on the train as I traveled east. I expected more. This is a miserable windy place. Rain peppers my back like needles, it might as well be sleet. It makes this Utah boy feel like he wants to be home. How I miss your apple turnovers!

Dora exclaimed, "Apple turnovers! He should have thought of that before he left. Turnovers, my foot."

Nannie took a seat next to Dora.

I wish you could be here to enjoy the fireworks display.

Aloud, Dora continued to share her reaction with Nannie. "I just wonder if he is watching the display with some lovely Eastern girl in the latest fashion, her arm in his!"

Anyway, I'm here and will get in the academy or die trying. Say, take more time than you do to write me. They (the letters) aren't one fifteenth long enough. Please oblige. Sincerely, Lou.

To Dora, the ending of the letter seemed tacked on. She shared the sentences one after another with increased rapidity with Nannie, who rolled from one side of the bed to the other at each new proclamation, in language at once flippant and stilted, as if he were writing to a kid sister.

"*Sincerely!* Outrageous!" Yet, Dora knew how he meant all of it. She knew his ways, and this was all bluff. She momentarily softened her appraisal. He soon would be homesick if he wasn't already, and she would not withhold her greetings flying to him. She did begin letters then misplaced them, finding them later on the next day, adding on snippets he might have an interest in, always rewriting to make sure they were perfect. Of course, maybe he didn't care about that; the details, her words telling him she waited for him, using her time to prepare for their wedding.

He had reacted rather explosively to her arch comment in one letter about the fact that he could be gone for four years, longer than a mission! "Tell me you will spend all summer here! Mound Fort is dull, dull, dull!" she had written.

November twenty-seventh. *Dear Pol, Sort of in a rush, but yesterday—, let's see— I called in the riding hall and watched the cadets. They would ride as fast as the horses could go, drop the reins, throw their leg over the brute's head,*

*and alight on their feet, later they got back on their mount
to jump fences and make all sorts of antics with their sabers.
It was very interesting and I enjoyed it very much. I do tend
to get worked up over details as you know, Pol.*

This was much too impersonal for Dora, as was the
following: *I suppose you are teaching as usual and visit
the teacher's association regularly. Hope you will pursue
all the little pleasures to be enjoyed and, now I have to run,
darling, more later, Lou.*

He did add more later but still not an intimate
exchange. Sometimes Dora hated Lou's device of flowery
talk, tongue in cheek but still not intimate, as if he were
saying the things for an audience.

After supper, he had filled in with, *Anyway make
the most of your time, Pol. Mental agony and torture far
exceeds in waste and feelings physical, so think as lightly
as possible on the dark side of affairs and remember to
dwell only on the bright and glorious hereafter.*

Dora shook her head and did not share this one with
Nannie.

The next letter sought to draw her even more into his
daily routine.

*We usually walk to the village for an hour or so then
return and study until 10 or 10:30. Then sleep. Here is an
example of my problems, one of 700 I think, which reads
thus . . . By mixing 5 lbs. of good sugar (is there bad sugar?)
with 5 lbs. worth of something else, worth 4 cents a pound.
. . . Well, you get the idea. Find the price of the two, you
can see these are very difficult and require a great deal of
thought and scratch paper to do the arithmetic calculations*

*necessary to compute same. A person must have a peace-
ful mind when he tackles studies and unless he hears from
those he loves often, why, he is just no good. I can't imagine
why I've received no letters from home but may get something when I go to school today. If I do, I'll write you again
and attach this. Love to your mother, Lou. PS., tell her to
take care of my love until I return when praise God, I hope
I can attend to her care, that's you, Pol, Lou.*

A week later Dora found discouragement as she read
of his activities in the brotherhood of single men. It was
only a partial letter, and Dora became little engaged in
Lou's fascination with life back East. She shared her frustration with Nannie, as they lay across the bed sketching
ideas for Dora's wedding dress.

"Listen to this, Nannie, . . . 'Someone or other showed
me all over Philadelphia that we could travel in three
hours and then he bade me an affectionate adieu and
success when we parted.' When have you ever heard Lou,
even with his flowery affectations, bid anyone an affectionate adieu?"

Dora then turned on her back holding the sheets of
paper at arm's length over her head as she discontinued
reading for a moment. "Nannie, do you think my sweetheart has left me for good? He's making friends left and
right. At least he doesn't mention any young ladies. I
suppose that should be some comfort." Dora continued
with the letter at hand. "Listen to this. 'I met a Jackson
Fleming who compelled me to stay over another day
in Philadelphia and visit the sights, and I picked up a

terrific guidebook. He wanted me to write him when I reach The Point. I've also got a staunch friend in New York.'"

"Nannie, what if he never comes home?"

Nannie's blank expression hinted this was beyond her experience, but Dora could see her sister was obviously riveted by Dora's predicament and awaited the next chapter in the romance. For now, Dora was relieved their sisterly bickering had lessened, and she was delighted to be under the same roof with Nannie to share her romantic turmoil.

Chapter Ten
Dora Goes to Town

Early in the spring of 1890, Dora began working at the library three days a week. She felt very business-like as she dressed in the morning, setting off to go to work. Viv accompanied her the first day to make sure she caught the proper car, and Dora's father made sure he himself met her as she traveled north after work. As time went on, her schedule allowed for a forty-five-minute lunch, when she scurried the short distance to The Broom, a newly opened hotel, to eat with May and Tillie. Dora guarded this new area of her life, not telling Lou, saving up the small amount she earned to allow for a wedding gift. She had already picked out the grey pearl tie tac as she browsed in Lewis Jewelers with Nannie.

An older woman who worked at the library accompanied Dora and a young lawyer to Block's, a popular diner, early in May. Dora observed many attractive young men hardly giving her a passing glance, involved as they were in their newspapers or talk referencing business trends in the city or upcoming elections and if Peery or young Walquist would seek a vacant court appointment. Dora's attention was caught by a young woman rushing to a nearby table of men, pointing to something in the newspaper she flourished in front of them. This brought quite a reaction from the others, but whether it involved a local or national concern, Dora couldn't say.

As Dora resumed her duties at the library that day, she mulled over the fact that Lou spent a lot of money on travel. She was horrified as he detailed friends traveling to Italy or France for the summer, worrying that the same option might occur to him. And perhaps Eliza would make such a wish a reality, if Lou were to persuade his mother to underwrite such a venture.

In Lou's next letter, the salutation being, *My Darling Girl*, he ignored every question Dora had put to him, failing to respond as well to a single thought she shared. She was incredulous. He quibbled over how few letters he had received from his mother or Joe or his other friends. How did he have time to ruminate on anyone but his future bride?

He wrote, *Yes, I'm indeed fortunate in meeting new people. I can't account for it myself but down in Memphis,* (What was he doing in Memphis?) *I had to wait hours for my train back.* He sounded fully petulant. *I had managed to get together for the holiday with Mathew Emory Tilden and his family, who hosted me for four days. Grand people.*

Had his ardor cooled? All these unfamiliar sayings and references were sending Dora into a tailspin. The last straw was his condescending tone about her account of visiting Lou's mother to pay a call. Dora might have shared with Lou how the call was stiff, the tea of some unknown flavor, and she fairly choked down the driest cakes she had ever been served anywhere.

He persisted in calling attention to her provincial activities by reminding her to be faithful and useful in her Sunday School duties. *And continue to perfect your routine of self-examination and atonement.*

Well, it was clear he didn't know what he was talking about and was too big for his britches. Yet he did think of their future together as he judged her to be *holy for a future existence, and we will be better, for your desire for perfection.*

But now she couldn't tell if there was a tease in play or not. *Your devoted, Lou, P.S. I stopped in St. Louis on my way east, that's where ma and pa got married.* Dora nearly wept at the staleness of that item. At the same time, she awaited the next letter in a frenzy. Each successive envelope was ripped apart for news detailing when Lou would head west.

Recently Lou had met a new friend, *a fine fellow, lives in Brooklyn, wants me to visit him before I head west.* At this point, Dora allowed the letter to flutter to the floor.

Even in Nannie's pregnant state, she was enthralled, imagining the appearance of this young man from far away Brooklyn. For Dora's part, she was fading in the west as Lou continued to be pulled the other way. But that just couldn't be true! There could never be any danger of him not returning.

Soon Dora wrote that Nannie had a new baby. She added without subtlety, *I yearn for life growing within me, as fruit of our love and our union. Do you think me brash, Lou? Yours, Dora.* As she reread the note, she reflected on her feelings for Lou. Had he changed? Her ardor for him had only grown.

Indeed, in a few more months, Lou was on his way home, having failed to make the grade in mathematics. Dora was ecstatic, Lou resigned.

The flutter of wedding preparations, wires, notes, phone calls between family members—the Budges, the Barlows, the Wilcoxes, and the Jensens—to say nothing of storekeepers in Ogden and Logan, all pushed into high gear. Messages involving fittings and flower arrangements sent Dora into a delightful spin. Tillie, May, Nannie, Lizzie and others—even Cora, Joe's wife—gave suggestions, but Jane Dinah held the reins steady with consultation from Eliza. Everyone involved strained toward the December date to end 1890 and signal an inexorable approach to a fruitful new century. But first came the party given by May and Tillie, an event to be treasured in memory.

The invitation was on heavy cream stock rimmed in gold.

Misses Tillie and May Wilcox

Requesting your company for Monday Eve,
November 26, 1890
at a private masquerade
to be given for their friends at Woodmansee Hall.
Positively no one admitted unless en masque.
Dancing— 8:30

The party was a swirl of music, flowers, and dance. Lou partnered Dora many times during the evening in the *Varsouvienne,* a Polish dance named after the French word for Warsaw, *Varsouvie*. It was Dora's favorite dance. Close for most of the steps, Lou obliged her, although of late he favored the waltz which took Dora's breath away, executed as it was by an energized Lou. Her green irides-cent dress had been bought by Eliza on a recent trip to Chicago. Crystal earbobs accented the sheen in the dress fabric. Eliza had seen to the alterations herself.

Dora kept two copies of the invitation for her album, one inserted in the gilt edged page, the other in folded tissue between the heavier leaves, where she would insert extra calling cards, wedding invitations and AT HOME cards sent in just a few weeks after the wedding. The wedding would be solemnized in the Logan Temple of the Church of Jesus Christ of Latter-day Saints, in Logan City, Cache County, Territory of Utah.

After the morning ceremony, the party took lunch at The Caine-Cardon House in Logan. Two formal pho-tographs were taken of the couple; then one, at Lou's insistence, of Dora alone, after she had changed into a smart green traveling suit. He said with a grin it would feature her fashionable dress and carriage. At this comment, Dora found it impossible to meet his gaze given his explicit definition sometime earlier of her carriage.

Lou had reserved two rooms at The Broom Hotel in Ogden for their first night. The couple waved to the well-wishers as they boarded the train to Ogden. Some of the guests opted to stay and visit with friends and family from Cache Valley, returning the following day. Alone for the first time as a married couple, they sat side by side enjoying each moment of the journey; all the while contemplating journey's end with the anticipation their wedding signified, especially after nearly a year's separation.

Dora fingered the handle of the new carrying case beside her on the seat. Inside lay a trousseau of peach-colored *crepe de chine* items, some selected by Eliza and ordered from St. Louis. Carefully tucked away in a side pocket were special gifts from Lou to be opened after they were alone in their rooms. He had wrapped the box of Jitzy perfume in rose tissue tied with a silver ribbon. He had purchased it in New York City as he made his way home after a year at West Point. In a tiny green box, a pair of diamond earrings in filigree settings would that night replace the pearl drops which Dora had worn for the wedding.

Lou had charged his twenty-year-old brother Joe with seeing that the rooms met his specifications. A bouquet of cream and pale peach roses and delicate greens placed on the sitting room table softened the stark Eastlake furniture. Joe, not given to more than matter of fact routine, warmed to his part in what seemed to him the most romantic escapade he had witnessed. Though married himself, such extravagance, let alone imaginative preparation, would never have occurred to him. Not having attended the Logan event due to his wife Cora's lying in, Joe was now not only included but pivotal in assuring, through these preparations, his brother's best possible entry into the marital state.

Part Two
Ogden Days

Chapter Eleven
At Home

Married in The Logan Temple, December 3, 1890,
At Home, 28TH Street east of Monroe,
on and after December 14, 1890.

The cream card of heavy stock was handsome, modeled after Tillie's suggestion and similar to her own announcement. The lettering was dignified, softened by a leafy embellishment framing the words AT HOME. This announcement of their married state was not a surprise to anyone after a courtship of eight years.

Friends and family made the trip from Ogden to Logan to visit the newly married couple; Eliza was resplendent in a dark blue suit of the latest cut, which overshadowed the more modest dress of Jane Dinah and Dora's sister Nannie.

After celebration of the New Year came a time of settling in, getting used to each other as a married couple, and the fact that for a time they would live with Eliza. Dora had not forgotten the letter Lou had shown her a few years before, in which Eliza had inferred that Dora's influence over her son was not to her liking.

So long had Dora and Lou been friends, and now married, still they were not together for what Dora had supposed would be all waking hours, apart from Lou's time at work. The reality was very different than what she had imagined. Since Eliza traveled, she insisted the young couple stay in her house while Lou worked on their new home next door. Lou sought to finish the construction, including the particular design elements he and his new bride wanted.

Dora arose with hardly a glance at the clock, Lou having left earlier for work. Eliza's housekeeper Delia would be out and about early, seeing to provisions and other matters left in her capable hands with Eliza's absence. The new bride felt relieved Eliza was away. Though aware the house was not hers, Dora resolved to keep it neat and clean. Beyond that, no incentive existed to do much else, though she routinely fluffed the sofa cushions, looking toward the time when her home next door would demand the same attention.

Once awake, Dora was content to stay in one of her flowered wrappers, choosing to have her coffee at a small desk. Her box of scalloped edged notes was before her, the familiar blue paper seal unbroken. This was the second box she had used, noting each gift with a thank you for the sender's thoughtfulness. Whether the gift was a piece of silver or china or linen, no matter if it came from Smalley's or Zions Cooperative Mercantile Institution—called ZCs by most shoppers—or Boyles Furniture; in all cases, Dora had a way of sending her usually sweet disposition along with the note. She especially acknowledged the hours of toil in the case of hand-worked table and bed linens.

However, before she began the task, she reached for a handful of clippings, recipes, and newspaper articles recommending proper modes of etiquette, fashion, and ever popular hints on being a successful wife and homemaker. She unfolded a small column on which a poem titled, "Before and After Marriage" appeared. Dora smiled in a self-satisfied way at the contrast as the author related the difference in her beloved as an anticipated mate and then, a known quantity at last, a husband with foibles exposed, who had to be reminded to wipe his muddy feet. Dora shook her head, unable to conceive of a time when the mundane would mar her vision of marital bliss, interacting day after day with the object of her affections and desire.

She smiled at the photograph of Lou in his West Point uniform which she had placed near the inkwell. The small walnut desk belonging to Eliza had been pushed into a hallway near a window. As Dora leaned back, a sigh escaped her. She would have preferred if Lou hadn't been sent north on business, "one week, ten days at the most, darling." Dora fervently hoped they would be in their own house before Eliza returned from Chicago.

She took up a carefully cut out newspaper column with several other copies clipped together. As she scanned the words, she couldn't resist reading it aloud, beginning with the dignified heading: "Jensen-Barlow Nuptials."

"A lovely wedding luncheon was held at the newly opened Caine-Cardon House, following the Logan Temple ceremony, hosted by Fanny Budge who is a cousin of Miss Barlow. The tables were decorated in a winter woods theme featuring fragrant pine cuttings. Streamers and bows of deep rose ribbon were artistically arranged on artificial snow. Miss Budge, a musician herself, engaged a string trio from Logan, adding to the ambience. Favors for the guests were supplied by Logan's finest, Hansen Confectionery, and consisted of miniature selections of their candies in small silver foil boxes tied with deep rose ribbon. The bride is a daughter of the Oliver Barlow family of Mound Fort. Mr. Jensen is the elder son of Eliza and L. J. Jensen Sr. The bridegroom is a businessman in Ogden formerly associated with David Kay. After local travel, the couple will be at home in Ogden after December 14."

The article had been written by Fanny Budge herself, and Dora smiled at each endearing phrase.

Dora finished gathering her papers, delaying the notes she needed to write and selecting instead a copy of *The Bostonians* from the bookcase. She resolved to read it in the coming weeks, possibly before Eliza's return, and replace it before it would be missed. Her mother-in-law's collection of books offered an ongoing supply of reading material for Dora, who was interested in the ones not expressly recommended by Eliza for Dora's betterment. She had targeted two she had not read, which if known by Eliza, would cause some embarrassment to

Dora. Eliza had reacted with a raised eyebrow at several omissions in Dora's reading history.

Her mother-in-law even had books in her bedroom, in a glass front case convenient to a sturdy chair and table before the fire. Dora could imagine a choice being made after a wearing day of travel and deliveries. She imagined the relaxation of escape into either a world of fiction or reviewing further information found in the various journals which came by mail. On the shelves were Latin texts, Pliny and Tacitus, side by side framing copies of the Bible and the Book of Mormon. Dora had not read Melville's *Typee* but noticed several novels of Dickens, Hardy, and a well-thumbed copy of Twain's *Library of Humor* published in 1888. Medical readers and references pertaining to midwifery and general surgery were less conveniently positioned, indicating that relaxation was what Eliza most sought here. A framed copy of her midwifery certificate hung above the case.

Some months later, Dora's hand reached for the latest letter from Lou as she sat at the desk. It was still too cold to move next door, which delayed Lou spending as much time there, when not on the road. This latest letter was enthusiastic, but it didn't mesh well with Dora's recent state of mind or physical condition. She suspected a pregnancy. In the abstract and before their marriage, all was in a dreamy future, as she would care lovingly for her family with Lou standing beside her. But at that very moment, she rose to hurry to the bath, nausea overwhelming her.

Now back at her desk, she held the note from Lou. Though the letterhead was on E. C. Farley paper, coal agents for Cache County, a card with Lou's information was pinned at the corner, L. J. Jensen Grain and Lumber. Dora smiled at the pride pinned there.

My dear wife: Can it be that nearly a year has passed since you became my legal bride? I counted on returning home about this time, but I have been unavoidably detained and can't say when I shall get back.

This was too business-like and the news unwelcome. As he went on about where else he had been—Brigham, Logan—Dora lost interest. At that moment, she didn't care if *it rained so hard Sunday that I could do nothing. I was detained to see a wheat man who had promised to see me in the morning, and, I just cut a deal on a thousand bushels and have bought a large quantity beside.*

I received a telegram from Joe at Brigham and have heard sometimes twice a day about you and am pleased that you are better.

This information was not quite accurate. As Dora sipped the lemon tea cooling in her cup, she reached for a single cracker, her one bite of food since noon the day before.

Well my love, I am rather lonesome here. I have not the same desire to court female company as in years gone by. Could it be we will be parents by next year? I hope so.

By this time tears were flowing. She sucked on another cracker that went down with ease.

Say, do you know what I've done? Well, at Brigham I used my nightshirt and as usual threw it at you, after taking it off, in my imagination, of course, but you were not there to put it under the pillow for me and when I went to don it at Logan, it had vanished. I conclude that some other fellow is using it now.

Then her beloved went on about cars of wheat and the names of places he traveled and camped. All became a blur.

When I shall reach home is a mystery, but our meeting will be all the more pleasant when I do return. Now do not want for anything. Joe is at your call and David Kay also. I must be going uptown and will say goodbye to my darling, Lovingly yours, Lou.

Chapter Twelve
Do Not Forget Me, Never

Rockport 8/25/91

Dearest, I came down today for mail, none, but I rec'd the pkg, thank you for your thoughtfulness. I needed the things. I spent last night washing and ironing.

Dora closed her eyes as she tried to blot out the view of her sweet boy taking care of himself and not even getting the note she wrote. How could it not be in the box? She found the letter where it had slipped behind the desk because of her haste and carelessness.

I am hauling the lumber we've been sawing, will have a carload soon and get a little credit. I wrote DK to pay you $15.00, can't say but probably he'll do it. He knows I'm good for it, hate to bother Viv just now and Joe wouldn't understand. Just ask him, darling.

Dora stiffened at this. She would rather ask Eliza than David. She didn't have the long history with him and besides Eliza, like it or not, was more privy to their finances. Lou wanting to be on his own, having been trained by David Kay, shouldn't mean that as a married couple they needed to go to him in an emergency.

Just go as you are, downtown, and stop in and ask if he's heard from me, just to be friendly.

As she was, she wore a most inappropriate outfit for going uptown. But she knew what Lou meant. It still sounded manipulative somehow. Of course, Lou would make it good when he returned. She read on.

When I ship the car, we will have to take merchandise for it and I am sure we can then pay for your mother's coal oil, flour and potatoes to carry through the winter. Tell her I will attend to any other business she requires. You say your father's sight is failing. I know Viv is too distracted with things in Denver to go back and forth. I'll borrow the money myself if I don't earn it. Could you ever believe things would be so complicated? Write me oftener. I know that's not a word but I get so lonely up here Pol, I go to the mill for a load at sunup and never see a face then for two weeks like this time, nothing, not a letter or paper, it is really tough. I could not endure this but for you and our little one coming, but I can make enough soon to carry us in provisions through the winter.

This was his duty for her, his kindness toward her mother, but so much would be easier if he were in Ogden. Could not men be hired to help him a bit to get the work done before the season changed? He again could sit at his desk in the store and be home with her at night. Dora realized her frustration was not from anger, only concern for him. She sensed a pattern forming that had the potential for weakening their marital bond.

Write me darling as often as you can, your letters fill my heart with intense yearning that is lovely, yes I write lovely, and sad. Dear one, I love you with all my mind and strength and my strength is increasing as I work. Look on that as a good thing, the better to hold you. So, do not forget me, never. I would come home but the weather is fine, my health good, and I must work for us. It is nearly five and must go to the ranch so I must stop, Lou.

The last was written with an attempt at a broad stroke of his pen, a skill he had developed as a young boy and later to court her.

Dora had kept every flowery message he had sent in the 1880s before they married, and true to her desire for neatness, returned each to its envelope. Before she slipped into bed that night, she would write him and have Mabel, the hired girl, post the letter, and she would bake something to send in the morning. How did her time slip away?

Earlier, she had seen two friends from the ward walking toward the house. As she rushed into the kitchen to tidy up a bit, she saw they had continued up the street, not stopping. She sank into a chair relieved somehow, feeling chastened by her Heavenly Father. She knew she should participate in ward activities. What was she doing after all that she couldn't write her beloved every day? A few lines, it wouldn't take much really; not to worry him with anything except her intense loneliness and the chilling concern that he would be hurt.

Chapter Thirteen
A Son in Ogden

After reading a newly arrived letter, Dora felt more at ease seeing how soon Lou was going to return. Eliza had traveled to Denver and was due back in less than a week. Dora replaced Eliza's copy of *The Bostonians* in the bookcase without reading more than a few chapters. She resolved to gather in her own home a collection of the newer writings of the day. She would frequent the downtown bookstore, what was it called? She struggled with the name—Harris, Hatch and Croft. She would stop by the store after her shopping was done, and if Mabel would mind the baby, after the baby came, to have time to browse the shelves and make her selections.

Her plans became out of reach almost as she uttered them.

Lou's return, happily before his mother arrived, gave a new focus for Dora beyond her pregnancy. Her loneliness was severe when he was gone. She had no energy even for preparing for the move next door, and though Eliza's housekeeper Delia's attentions were substantial,

Dora wanted to run her life and home, and to be Lou's "all in all," as she had once written in a letter.

The move was accomplished amid the usual entanglements of misplaced items and the unplanned breakage of two priceless figurines, priceless to Dora since they had been given to her by her mother, brought from her native Italy. Dora dissolved in tears as she told Delia about her loss but in truth, there was little emotional cost. Delia shook her head at times as Dora wavered between self-aware poise and a total dependence on Lou as her anchor.

Dora thought of a few other touches which Lou added, as he arranged new furniture from Boyles. Joe donated several hours of painting with help from the Harris boys. In fact, that held up the move because of the fumes. Finally, Eliza, sure that the harmful nature of the paint had dissipated, allowed the move. But in truth, Dora's frequent headaches increased due to the strong-smelling paint and varnish. Medically injurious or not, thorough airing of the rooms was necessary before Dora could sleep overnight in her new feather bed with Lou.

Being in her new home was all she dreamed of as the couple talked long into the night, having the privacy at last to know each other in a new way. Dora's body had changed and Lou, so often away, was caught off guard at the recent weeks' changes. Fascinated at the development which Dora had grown accustomed to, the growth during a pregnancy was beyond his knowledge. He would never have dreamed of asking his own mother for specifics, though she might have sought to convey accurate information to her son. Now his willing teacher was his own wife.

⌒

Their first son, whom they named Jesse, was two weeks late according to Eliza but fine in every way. Her hand was less than steady as she filled in the particulars for the county record, but then no one was looking over her shoulder to see this slippage of her usual professional behavior. Line after line reading upward on the page listed her as having delivered the children for the Harleys, the Richardsons, the Perrys, the Crofts and the Munsons, but this notation of her first grandchild surpassed all the rest. She beamed with satisfaction at her signature on the same line with Louis Jesse Jensen.

Dora could see that Lou was captivated by the glossy dark curls on his boy, so like her own. She was expecting a bald-headed baby, something of a tradition in the Jensen family so she was told, but no complaint came from Lou. Dora's care beyond initial clinical needs was thorough. Delia outdid herself cooking for Lou, sending him off having had an adequate breakfast. Dora was given over to Eliza, Delia and Mabel Stokes, a hired girl often employed by Eliza. Delia dispatched each in turn to fetch cool drinks, which the new mother craved; and Dora was not unaware of the special attention Mabel gave to put all in order in Dora's home.

In less than ten days, Lou was on the road again, this time a letter arriving from Rockport. Dora wasn't even sure where this newest camp was.

Dear Dora, I guess you can see I'm in Rockport, a not too primitive camp, and could you send up some preserves?

Was this supposed to make her feel better, more secure, or sorry for him? She had no knowledge of Rockport and never intended to go there if she could help it. Hot and rocky, how else could she imagine it? Dora wanted him home. She was numb to the recitation of sawn wood, loaded cars and lumber, lumber, lumber! She could fairly smell it. Then an earnest and business-like request for her to see David Kay about an additional helper. Surely Dora was supportive of that accommodation since Lou talked of dark coming on before he returned to the mill. She could scarcely visualize the conditions of his daily routine. Was it worse than she imagined or not terribly more difficult than rugged camping? Then back to the preserves and she smiled at his rash boyishness.

You can rake up (well, not really rake!) a can for the preserves. Oh yes, you know I bought you a tin screw top can, that's the thing, take and leave it at mother's and the new man can bring it up and if you can, call Joe and find out for certain the date of deer killing, could you? There is nothing else now, take good care of Jesse, I know you don't need telling but it shows my interest. That didn't come out quite as I planned! I'm a little goofy, hungry and tired. Love yourself and our son, I will love both when I get home again, Lou.

As she read, Jesse was at her breast. Certainly, the needs and requests from Lou would have her utmost attention. Mabel would adequately pack the tin with some additional canned goods, and Delia would see to the mailing chore. She wanted it to reach Lou long before the new man found the time to travel.

In the morning Dora often sat on a stool at the front kitchen window. She set her mug, one of the ones Lou preferred, on the counter provided by a pine step-back cabinet, the roomy workspace to her liking for rolling out pie crusts. It was only slightly worn, but there was a decidedly unattractive burn mark near the edge, close to where she now sat. Lou often rested his cigarette on the edge if he were called by her to reach an item on the top shelf, or lift up a heavy, seldom-used bowl for safe storage.

Dora discouraged his smoking, reminding Lou of the church's teaching, including Word of Wisdom guidelines pertaining to his coffee drinking. Dora stressed the obedience aspect but when that didn't seem to work, pivoted to the health issue. "Lou, I know you wouldn't be so jumpy at times if you limited your daily coffee." At that point, Lou raised his hands in a surrender pose smiling broadly.

There were instances where she made compromises. Dora would raise the window noisily; and he would comply with her wishes, stubbing out his cigarette and making sure it was safely in the trash bin. Just now however, as she sat there, she traced the burn mark with her thumb and missed Lou's presence. A robin's song outside as she raised the window gave back the beauty of her heartache.

How differently things seemed to be from what she and dear Tillie had envisioned just a few years before. Rocking her son, Dora looked down with pride at her firstborn, remembering so many girlhood conversations she and Tillie had engaged in, speculating on motherhood and day to day life with their sweethearts. Never destined to be won by Joe, Tillie had become engaged to Lyman Peck, nearly six years older. At her mother's urging, the wedding had taken place in the Manti Temple located some two hundred miles south of Ogden. In fact, Lou and Dora were traveling north of Ogden at the time and they were unable to attend the wedding. Tillie and Lyman had soon afterward moved to Saint George in southern Utah, the warmest area of the state, even in winter. Her doctor had deemed it better for her health, which was delicate and had been even when the girls were in school. Though Dora tried to keep up a correspondence with her once ebullient friend, return notes were short and stiff. However, the memory of the party given for Lou and Dora before they wed, never dimmed. Dora had pressed the lovely party invitation in her scrapbook as well as some of the many notes from Lou which Tillie had faithfully delivered to Dora over the years of their long courtship.

Chapter Fourteen
Man about Town

Lou often took the trolley to work, enjoying the vibrancy of Ogden's downtown scene. More often than not, he hopped off, impatient to set his own pace.

Lou's lanky frame moved with purpose north on Washington Avenue. He had left the courthouse where he was clerk an hour before and more recently had emerged from The Broom where he had received a shave, trim and shoeshine. He had been trying once again to grow a mustache, but with Dora's discouragement, and his uneven ability to do so, the project was abandoned. He and his wife didn't see hair growth, after all, as a sign of virility as did some sporting full beards in addition to mustaches. More importantly, he was satisfied with his current fashion appearance. The latest addition to his attire was a pair of Hanan shoes purchased from C.D. Ives, a new haberdasher, whose store was part of The Broom Hotel shops.

After pausing a few moments to chat with Fred Kiesel, Ogden's first non-Mormon mayor, who, Lou thought, was impeccable in his dress, he resumed his train of thought, considering his contribution to the uptown tapestry where he felt secure. Although not as prominent as some, he was at least respectable and well liked.

This morning Lou set a brisk pace in the sunny but cool late morning air. He darted across the street to enter Blocks for a cup of coffee and roll, along with a brief glance at the papers. He eased onto a stool at the counter, bumping one knee as he did so. After choosing a copy of *The St. Louis Post-Dispatch* and one other Eastern paper, he mulled over a recent comment attributed to Mark Hanna following the McKinley assassination: "Now that damn cowboy is in The White House," referring to Theodore Roosevelt. Lou was ashamed at the unbidden chuckle that escaped him; but, in fact, Lou and many of his friends were pleased by the new President's vitality and purpose.

Lou felt it important to keep abreast of national goings on. He was not immune to the glances of others in Blocks as they noticed him perusing the editorial comments with furrowed brow. On the other hand, his primary concerns, written large in his heart, were Dora and Jesse. Governmental gyrations seemed far away earlier that morning as he had gazed at the eastern bounds of his world; the Wasatch mountains which framed each day's beginning, golden this time of the year, silver-crested in time, with the winter's snow.

Hastily Lou slipped from the stool, returning the papers to their assigned rack. He decided to forgo a roll, fueled instead by the mug of black coffee automatically poured for him as he had sat down. He checked his pocket watch, lifted his hat from the hook and with a wave to Mrs. Block, exited the popular establishment.

As Lou passed the familiar store fronts, he looked forward to the new sign he was having installed over the entrance to his business. His own workers were doing the lion's share of the work, with an expert painter to execute the message, L. J. Jensen and Bros. Soon after his marriage, Lou had decided to strike out on his own after having been a protégé of David Kay since he was a boy. Lou was unstintingly grateful, so much so that he resolved his next son would be named David Kay Jensen, an intention he had postponed with his first son in deference to Dora's wishes.

Lou's brother Joe was a hard worker; and the family bond, the two sons working as a team, bolstered by his mother's backing, was strong. His brother-in-law Vivian Barlow, Dora's younger brother, being more schooled in legal procedure, became a trusted unnamed partner. Though not a lawyer in fact, Viv was able to guide the Jensen brothers through the more technical aspects of running their own company efficiently. In time, Joe would shoulder the more physical aspects of the work, which he preferred, and Lou, especially after Viv moved to Denver, would assume the office presence, keeping an eye on the very areas Viv had identified.

Lou crossed the street mid-block, tipping his hat as he passed two female acquaintances from the court. Lou freely bestowed his infectious grin on other shopkeepers as he caught their eye. Shopkeepers habitually stood in front of their doors to gauge the traffic and entice possible customers; one man always vigorously swept the area just in front of his entrance. After two or three congratulatory waves from friends who acknowledged his new son as well as the new sign, Lou entered the dim shop.

Viv, at the roll top desk in the rear, held a fistful of papers, likely bills and invoices. Their work for the remainder of the day would revolve around deciphering their financial situation. Viv had argued against the new sign, suggesting instead a late fall date for installation, but had yielded to his brother-in-law's enthusiasm. This part of the business was less to Lou's liking. His strong suit was working on the phone, his feet up on the desk, an eye on the calendar for promising dates of delivery, then following through with good service for his particular clientele.

Lou, at one time, had wondered if starting a wholesale grocery in direct competition with David Kay, along with selling lumber, would be feasible now.

He learned the wholesale grocery business from David Kay, who, as his mentor, had trusted him with responsibilities beyond his years. Lou had benefitted so much that now he was confident in making this change. David had encouraged him and was pleased to see the sign down the street from his own store. Lou's business would concentrate on lumber, other building materials and supplies, rather than wholesale groceries, but offer housewares in addition. Both men, the senior Kay and Lou, were of the opinion that there was business enough to go around, even with economic gyrations which had been felt. The building and outfitting of new homes in Ogden was a tangible sign of prosperity in the future.

Recently Fred Kiesel had offered him a job in his much larger wholesale grocery business. It was tempting, and he certainly knew the range of stock, but this would put him in direct competition with David. Besides, Mr. Kiesel had intimated that a relocation would be part of the offer and Lou wasn't interested in a move and he knew Dora's heart without even asking her.

Lou's new friend Frank Elgin, first met through the Elks fellowship, advised Lou to write out an objective list of future expectations, including deficits as well as evaluating future growth. Frank was a lawyer who had relocated from St. Louis. At first Lou was taken aback at the sober tone, but he appreciated Frank's realistic appraisal. Frank had also mentioned that he was a vestry member at Good Shepherd Episcopal Church, located a few blocks west on Grant Avenue. In this office, members were tasked with seeing to the fiduciary needs and requirements of the parish. The rector was involved, in addition to worship, in more pastoral concerns. Since Frank had a keen knowledge of the area's economic potential, he could, as appropriate, put in a good word for Lou and his business.

Frank, therefore, suggested that Lou take advantage of the asset of space over the store for rental, an arrangement which would add financial support. The location was excellent and, according to Frank, needed just a small investment in cleaning and painting. New tradesmen, especially those setting up new businesses, might find the location perfect as well as economical, before committing to a larger residential property.

Lou had been using the space for haphazard storage having nothing to do with the business. Space had been made available to friends who needed a place, "Just temporarily, Lou, while I get things sorted out. You know how business has been the last few months. Not for everybody but . . . . You know me, Lou, I'm good for it."

Regardless of the reason for the request, Lou never said no.

As Lou entered his office, the phone jangled and, now in place at his desk, he reached for it.

Later, having dealt with a customer's issue in an ingratiating manner, Lou leaned back in his chair and wondered if Dora was truly pregnant again. She couldn't be but what if she was? Maybe he would do well to accelerate plans to add to his income with the rental space. Elbows on his desk, he cradled his head in his hands. Jumping up he grabbed hat and coat, making for the door, saying out loud, "I've got to get home."

Chapter Fifteen
Annie

The sign over one of the newer stores in Ogden, advertised *Annie Elgin, Millinery*.

A smaller card propped on an easel in the window gave further information:

Hats trimmed in the latest fashion.

For Dora's first outing after Jesse's birth, Lou had accompanied her downtown. Dora, excited to go to town, especially with Lou at her side, had chosen her outfit with care, the bodice made by Eliza to allow for her slightly larger bosom. A glance in the mirror as she left home confirmed to her that the sparkle she felt as Lou's wife and mother to their first son had not diminished. Jesse was safe in Eliza's care for the afternoon and, with Delia in attendance, Dora knew both Eliza and Delia would try to outdo each other fussing over the baby.

Eliza had specified ecru trim for yet another bodice she was making for Dora and had sketched the exact design. She had sent the couple to the new shop owned by the sister of Frank Elgin, a new lawyer in town. Dora knew Frank was a recent acquaintance of Lou's, having heard from her husband that Annie and Frank had moved from St. Louis and both found Ogden welcoming; the legal community, enhanced by Frank's credentials and experience, and the commercial area only too happy to include a stylish millinery run by a lady from "back East." Annie, a shop owner of some experience, had learned her craft at Marshall Fields in Chicago.

Dora was interested in reviewing the goods carried in the shop and also curious to meet a maiden lady in business for herself. A delicately lettered sign over one counter informed customers that, "Weekly arrivals from Chicago and St Louis are standard. Madeline Anne Elgin, Owner."

Dora and Lou entered the store, finding it light and airy, unlike many other establishments. Fresh flowers occupied vases on the counters. Colorful fabric panels hung on attractive brackets. Wood moldings framed several mirrors which reflected the display cases. Trellises in front of storage alcoves hid them from view. A small seating area had been decorated with potted palms.

The couple was greeted at once by the owner herself. "Hello, Lou, Frank has told me so much about you. We were quickly introduced in front of Blocks just last week." She clasped Lou's hand briefly as she turned toward Dora. "And this must be Dora, a new mother, how lovely." Dora and Lou exchanged a very private glance.

After the three sat down, Annie nodded as Dora described her needs, showing her Eliza's sketch. In less than fifteen minutes, the trim was measured and wrapped and, to Dora's delight, cost less than twenty-five cents.

As Annie wrapped the trim, Dora noticed two small embroidered samplers on the wall behind her. Side by side they bracketed a small vase on a decorative shelf.

When Dora asked about them, Annie said, "They are two of my favorite sayings and I try to keep them uppermost in my mind. When I feel a bit lazy and doubt my abilities, I focus on 'Neglect not the gift that is in thee.' Of course, to stave off discouragement, the Galatians quote has no parallel: 'Be ye therefore not weary in well doing for in due season, ye shall reap if ye faint not.'" Annie laughed. "Putting those words in modern usage finds them just as effective, and they urge me on."

With a pat on the small parcel on the counter, she seemed to Dora as satisfied as if the sale had been for five dollars. Lou had made his exit a few moments before, promising to return within the hour.

As Lou sped along the walkway, he turned over in his mind the possibility that Dora might in truth be with child. Dora, in a furtive conversation as they were preparing for bed the night before, shushed the idea emphatically. But still . . .

Back in the millinery, all was ladies gently getting to know each other, the business setting. "I hope you don't consider me forward as a businesswoman not addressing you as Mrs. Jensen. Ogden is such a friendly community and we get to know each other more informally. At least I have found it that way."

"Oh no, quite the contrary," Dora replied. "Your brother, Frank, and Lou are already friends and I hope we shall be as well."

Dora rose, pulling on her gloves, glancing at a delicate Christening dress in a nearby glass case.

Noticing, Annie asked, "Can I show you something else, Dora?"

Dora considered the purchase for Nannie's new baby. The blessing was scheduled in less than two weeks and she had volunteered to find something Nannie would like that could be used by subsequent offspring. Surely the stunning gown would be appropriate. Eliza had insisted on buying the gown used for Jesse's blessing. Dora considered that she might have reason to use it again within a few months.

Still she hesitated. The price tag was difficult to read, and Dora didn't want to put on her glasses; although the glasses were visible to others, attached to a delicate chain pinned to her shirtwaist. The dress might cost more than she could pay; she would consult with Lou first.

"I feel just a bit tired now, and I see Lou just a half a block away." She squinted in the general direction of the front window. "Another time I'll see to it. I'll have a good excuse to return, and we can deepen our friendship." The comment was friendly but proper and without a stiffness Dora allowed in most commercial interactions.

As Dora left, she picked up a card from the counter: *Madeline Anne Elgin, Millinery—Trousseaux our specialty, items ordered by wire, discretion honored.*

～

Two weeks later, Annie hailed Dora on the northeast corner of 24th and Washington Avenue. Dora returned the wave. Annie's arm was through that of her brother Frank, who she introduced to Dora as they came together. The three moved south while chatting informally, then deciding on pie and coffee at Blocks. As they walked easily along, Frank positioned himself nearest the street curb, Annie next to her brother. Dora leaned forward slightly, noticing Frank's dress and carriage. Not as tall as Lou but dignified, tipping his hat as the trio passed Kibby Malan and Fanny Mattsson. Lou would have done the same, but of late he might have been too preoccupied to respond with a tip of his hat, a warm smile and "Good afternoon, ladies," as Frank did.

Chapter Sixteen
Coffee with Frank

The two men had agreed to meet at Frank's early on Saturday afternoon. Lou had walked up from his store downtown, finding the 25th Street hill no challenge since he was fit and also curious about Frank's living arrangements. As he turned the corner at Jefferson, he waved to Frank who stood in front watching for him.

As the two men met, they shook hands heartily. Lou was dressed for business, as he had just been in the store, his one nod to informality the removal of his coat as he sat at his desk. He had worn the jacket for his meeting with Frank, who wore slightly rumpled trousers of the type one might wear on a canyon excursion. A rough sweater was topped by an olive corduroy jacket which strained across Frank's broad shoulders.

Lou said, his breath visible, "I supposed you lived with your sister Annie."

"No, she rooms with the Elgars from Good Shepherd. Rodney and I are on the vestry, fine chap. They were glad to have someone like Annie living with them after their two daughters married and moved away. Of course, you know Annie, she brightens any corner and can pay better rent than most. Actually, Annie moved here before I made arrangements for my own relocation."

The two men turned to walk toward the handsome building facing the park. They moved slowly, enjoying the sun on their backs.

"My older brother Crawford traveled out this way while I was still in school," Frank continued. "He loved the country but, of course, would miss the big city life. Besides, his wife Edythe wouldn't hear of it, and his children are getting a superior education there in St. Louis."

Frank removed a key from his jacket pocket as they walked up the sandstone stairs to the porch. He inserted the key in the lock of one of the oak double doors. They entered a bright entry hall which smelled of lemon wax.

The building housed four roomy apartments. The front door on the left was Frank's, and as Lou entered, he felt as if he had traveled east to Philadelphia or New York, where he had visited friends during his short time at West Point. There was a faint aroma of cigar or pipe smoke and the unmistakable smell of old books, carpets and well-oiled furniture. Frank's living room overlooked the park.

After hanging up their coats by the door, Frank indicated a comfortable pair of leather chairs placed before the fireplace. Hardly had the two settled themselves, before Frank jumped up. "I'll just get the papers for the rental above your store from my study. I've got coffee,

Lou. I know you like a cup." The words trailed off as he moved down the hall. ". . . Whatever the time of day."

Lou stood to scan the walls and shelves. Watercolors, nudes, urban scenes in oil, and sketches of the Western desert were interspersed with small bronze figurines and coarse pottery which Lou could not identify. On the shelves he recognized works by Hugo, Cooper, Shakespeare, and Tarkington, although most titles were unfamiliar to him. In a large basket between the chairs was an assortment of magazines, *Field and Stream, Motoring Trends for Today, Vacations Westward,* and well-thumbed copies of *McClures,* featuring *The Gentleman from Indiana* in serialized form.

"Here you are, Lou, strong to your liking, and some rich date bread from Annie. Personally, I prefer Mrs. Block's orange nut bread." Frank placed a tray with cups and plate on a low table near the chairs.

"First, let's get this out of the way. Just sign here and here." He indicated with a jab of his finger, handing Lou a handsome pen. Continuing his train of thought, Frank said, "I have looked over this rental agreement carefully, didn't have to do much. Viv had all the particulars right. Fine fellow, think he'll move to Denver? I hope not. Heard his wife runs the show, just remember lots of black taffeta. She in mourning?" Frank laughed and shook his head. "Don't mean that to be humorous if she is."

"No, but I agree she's not given to color," Lou said but didn't add more, concentrating on the hot coffee after signing the papers. He drank slowly. It was excellent, better than Blocks, which was considered the best in town. He chose his words carefully, running his thumb across his jaw. "Just trying to get a feel for the kind of things that interest you, Frank." His gaze took in the whole room. "This is another side of you from what I see at Elks meetings and our time up at Burton French's place in the canyon."

"Well," Frank looked up and smacked his lips, "I'm fortunate to have had the opportunity to collect what pleases me."

Lou walked over to examine a sketch which hung at eye level. It was of the Chestnut Street Bridge in Philadelphia. He had no trouble identifying it. This was something which interested him in a more practical way. He had walked over that very bridge and admired it from a builder's perspective. He had noted in his guidebook, "path-walk nicely paved with slate flagging."

Frank broke into his thoughts. "You know Philadelphia, Lou?"

"Just there once on my way back west from New York." He felt the color rise to his cheeks. He would rather not discuss why he had returned to Utah in 1890. Lou examined the drawing more closely and noticed that Frank was the artist. "A nice likeness, Frank."

"Thanks, Lou. I love to sketch, haven't had a lot of time to give to it lately." He pivoted slightly, pointing to two oils on the left. "These are by John Willard Clawson, a Utah artist. He was at the Ecole Des Beaux Arts in Paris, studied with Manet and Monet. His wife is a daughter of Brigham Young, believe it or not." Frank chuckled.

Lou's eyebrows raised. Now this was a bit of trivia he could share with Dora if he remembered the name of the artist.

"I'm lucky to have these two landscapes. The man moved recently to San Francisco, a loss for Utah I'd say."

Lou, feeling out of his element, was struck by the off-handed way his friend had shared his knowledge. "Well, I'd better get on. Dora will be expecting me." As he pulled on his coat, he saw a copy of Theodore Dreiser's *Sister Carrie* on the hall table. Without much thought, he said, "Sister Carrie, like sister Annie."

Frank winced but smiled good naturedly at Lou's comment.

"Go ahead, take it, Lou. Dora might enjoy it. Quite a slice of life." Lou took the loan as a sign of his friend's generosity. He himself was unfamiliar with the book and only hoped it was appropriate for his wife.

Lou's head was spinning as he walked away from Frank's apartment. The things he didn't know, Manet, Monet, what was the difference? A Utah artist studying in Paris? He wondered if Dora had ever heard of John Willard . . . he'd forgotten the name already. Anyway, Dora's pies were better than Annie's date bread. And here he was with a red leather-bound copy of a book by Theodore Dreiser just for her to read. He quickened his pace in the colder air. The sun dimmed for the day and the last few blocks east then south would be stepped off, quickly.

Chapter Seventeen
1893, at Home

Dora deferred to Eliza, Lou's mother, especially since they lived with her before their house next door was finished. She tried to feel affection for Eliza but was guarded. Taken aback by Eliza's attempts at humor, Dora found some of her comments coarse.

"I've had thirty-six babies this month!" Eliza said, adding, "It's a matter of record, Dora, there is nothing shocking about the deliveries I perform." Eliza smiled at her daughter-in-law, and patted her lightly on the back.

Lou, observing this, winked at his wife as he sipped his coffee.

Because Eliza was a midwife, household routine, even in Dora and Lou's home, was influenced by her opinions about diet and exercise. At times, even the type of footwear, bedding, length of sleeping hours, and amount of exposure to the sun came under her watchful eye.

Lou assured Dora that after their move, the new Jensen household would operate as she decided. If Dora wanted a vase of autumn leaves or a bowl of lilacs or even a platter of rocks from the canyon on display, none of her decorating decisions would be criticized. Secure in this, Dora pressed to make her home an intermountain model of taste and warmth.

Dora was particularly proud of her dining room. She basked in the glow of her friends' positive comments. The walnut sideboard had a marble top. Over it hung a simply framed mirror. Five side chairs were placed around the table, each at a slight angle to encourage seating. Eliza always pushed them into the table as if she were inconvenienced by Dora's bit of invention. An additional chair with a high back and sturdy arms was reserved for Eliza. Dora had ordered a dark tapestry fabric to cover the chair cushions from a company in Philadelphia. She had seen the advertisement in the guidebook Lou had saved from his travels East. He himself often thumbed through it for ideas, brim full of current information about stores and companies. Many offerings from back East were available by special order.

Maple flooring in the dining room lay underneath the carpet. Several layers of newspapers between the carpet and the floor provided padding and protection. Each fall, Dora directed Lou and his brother Joe in the removal of tacks, pulling up the carpet and very carefully transferring it to the rear of the property. Here the rug was shaken and beaten until no flecks of soil remained. Much had been ground in during the summer. Lou was not always aware of how much soil could cling to his soles.

Lou had made sturdy racks for carpet cleaning, not to endanger the more fragile clothes lines. Often this process took the better part of the day since Lou and Joe stopped to read the papers previously read many months before, as they moved across the floor on their hands and knees. Dora cautioned them to move slowly so as to avoid stirring up dust but checked often on their progress, urging them to keep at their task.

Dora became extremely testy this time of the year. She couldn't abide disorder, and the noise and confusion of moving furniture, taking down drapes and moving carpet invariably caused her sick headaches, often accompanied by episodes of undeserved fault finding, which she knew disturbed Lou. This change in her usually pleasant disposition led to still more teasing from her husband, who happily put everything back together.

Order finally achieved, her thank you would take the form of a favorite meal: pork roast with blistered potatoes and homemade apple sauce, with rice pudding for dessert served from a cut-glass bowl, the tops of the rich treat crusted with brown sugar and a rim of heavy cream around the edge.

Dora had a few good quality linens that she used on Sundays to set her table for a generous early afternoon meal. Eliza came most Sundays for dinner and had made comments about the fussiness of Dora's style of house décor, especially table settings. This particular night Dora had served stewed chicken, fresh peas, potatoes, her homemade rolls and a dollop of heavy cream for

Eliza's coffee. Lou was traveling and had last called from Shoshone Idaho.

After dinner the two women sat in front of the fire. Dora was nursing the baby. Soon Dora left her chair, moving to a room down the hall. Jesse would sleep next to her, settled between the couple when Lou came home. Dora had just sat in her chair, and was in the process of handing Eliza a shawl she had requested, with a motion of her hand.

Jarring the stillness like a bolt of thunder, riders approached with the sound of hoof beats. If the women had been on the porch, they would have seen the horses pulled tight at the rein by two riders who dismounted in great haste. Frenzied banging on the door summoned both women. Dora drew the bolt, always used when Lou was away. The men stood there as lathered as their horses and spoke the words which drove much of Eliza's life: "The doctor."

"Get these men some water, Dora," Eliza instructed. Her mother-in-law questioned them while Dora ran to get the water. When she returned, the men sank down on the steps, removed their hats and drank noisily.

Eliza moved quickly to the dining room. She yanked opened drawers, removing Dora's prized linens, shaking out the tablecloths to assess which were usable. She then ripped them into strips for bandages.

A man had been caught in farm machinery and his brother, attempting to help him, was also injured. Their sons had come to Eliza after trying without success to reach surgeons in town, one of whom had gone to Boston.

"The wagon is too slow," Eliza said. "You men ride double and I'll take the larger horse with my supplies."

They didn't question her authority. "Fetch Lou's pants!" she said to Dora, who meekly reached for the work pants on a hook on the porch. With some urgency, she called, "No, the grey wool ones, they're bigger. And my hat!"

Eliza unceremoniously stepped out of her skirt, drawing on the heavy pants as well as the long johns still inside them. She threw a canvas coat around her shoulders like a cape before pushing her arms through the sleeves. A pair of heavy socks followed, then Lou's boots. She stomped noisily on the porch as if to accentuate her decision to appropriate them for her own use.

"I may be gone for several days. I won't leave 'til they're out of danger." She laid a tender hand on Dora's shoulders. "The injured men were in my handcart company, and they are in a very isolated area, liable to have infection by the time I get there. I'll send this young man," she nodded toward one of the young men, "back for anything else I need."

Finally, Eliza swept from the room, her shoulder dislodging a drapery panel which she stepped on as she left.

As threads of cotton clung to Dora's hair, and the chandelier still jiggled crazily from the buffeting it had endured as Eliza shook out the larger tablecloths, Dora sobbed into her apron.

∽

Before the end of the week Lou returned, first getting the news of the event by phone. By now, Dora viewed the episode in a more logical perspective. But for her part, Eliza had returned as if nothing had happened, resuming her place at the table for Sunday dinner.

Dora was less talkative than usual. This woman had disrupted her household and she was now on guard for future events. She was unsure as how to handle a similar assault but as her eyes met Lou's, she didn't signal warmth and engagement, let alone intimacy.

⌒

From his copy of *Philadelphia Today,* Lou had ordered a new tablecloth augmenting some of the smaller linens with purchases from ZCMI. His repair of the drape bracket and Delia's vigorous dusting had restored the dining room to order in an afternoon, complete with flowers from the florist for the table.

As the family dined one evening, soon after Lou's return, Jesse warmed to his father's presence telling of school happenings and asking for a new book, anything having to do with science or as Dora termed it, pretend science. "Some of what you read, Jesse, will never happen. People up in the sky, in ships! Those stories about the future are outlandish! Papa, set your son straight."

Jesse winked at Lou. They knew better.

Later in their room, Lou chided Dora for referring to him as papa. "But Lou, in front of the children and you know, your mother."

"Have you ever heard my mother call me papa?" He grinned.

"No, of course not, but still . . ." Knowing his reaction would be right on the mark, her heart fluttered with some anticipation.

Lou picked her up in his arms as easily as if she were Jesse and plopped down in an easy chair holding her on his lap. In his grave but beguiling tone, he said, "Always call me Lou. Remember, I'm not your papa."

He rose, tossing her easily in the middle of their feather bed, which she had fluffed that morning as always. Holding first one corner then the others in turn, Dora had yanked the quilt up and down until she was satisfied with the puffed up result. Laying the broom handle across the bed lightly, not to press down and decrease the loft, Dora smoothed the surface from the foot to the headboard, where four large pillows crowned the effort. She had smiled at the perfection.

Now all was happily deflated as Lou energetically collapsed beside her, taking great pleasure in her body, changed after Jesse's birth.

Dora's new anticipated pregnancy had surprised Eliza, who believed a nursing mother couldn't become pregnant. Lou had been overjoyed at the news, and with Dora experiencing few early symptoms, decreed it would be a pregnancy of just a few months rather than the customary nine.

Dora Vivian, thereafter called Darling, was born without difficulty, to everyone's delight, Lou especially finding a new robust confidence in providing for his family, if, for a few weeks at least, financial worries led to noticeable preoccupation.

Chapter Eighteen
Sally

Mary Ellen Jensen was born on December 18, 1894. As was the case with Lou's other children, the event occurred at home on 28th Street, presided over by his mother. A few days later as he looked down at his new daughter, he rubbed his chin, commenting, "You know, I've always liked Sally for a name." Though his mother had recorded the name Mary Ellen Jensen in the county register, Sally was the name called and tried out by all, though Lou alone overheard his mother's mumbled, "If she's to be Sally, just name her Sally."

Lou, if not found at home or in his office, was seen glad handing Ogden citizens as if he were running for office. He accepted their congratulations as they came his way for weeks afterward. Only one acquaintance lamented the fact of "another girl, sorry, Lou," which ignored altogether the fact that the couple's first child Jesse was most certainly male.

In Lou's opinion, Dora appeared more robust since Darling's delivery and was able to nurse Sally without difficulty. Lou beamed to see his wife prop her feet on a small stool to better admire the new carpet slippers he had given her. One afternoon, as he finished his lunch prepared by Mabel, he overheard Eliza telling a friend on the phone that, "Delia is a true veteran, adept at lying in care, and she can cook too, not like I can, of course," she tittered in an uncharacteristic way. Lou found it somewhat reassuring that his mother was capable of light conversation. "In fact, Louise, she handles callers, listens to patients' complaints. Why, let me tell you that the day Sally was born, even with all the turmoil that can bring, nonetheless, she shifted the beginnings of the family's dinner, parsnip fritters with lamb stew, to the icebox and served it later all heated up! What do you think of that?" Eliza fairly barked into the phone receiver.

Lou beamed as he introduced Jesse to yet another sister. Lou intended to be more attentive to his son, after all, their interests would be very different in the future from those of the girls. If the boy felt disappointed, he disguised it completely. Lou reiterated that the two girls were outside any circle of interest, which the males in the family shared. "Jesse, you know the girls will have to be read to for the next few years." As Lou continued in an almost conspiratorial manner, his son nodded solemnly. "Jesse, I'm sure I can count on you to read, oh, for example The Bird's Christmas Carol or something similar to Darling especially. I know, son, that it is beyond your current interests, science and all," Lou slipped an arm across Jesse's frail shoulders, "but you know your mother will count on you." Lou's enquiring expression was met with a more energetic nod from his son. A smile completed the exchange between father and son. Catching Lou's eye and with a tug on his arm, Jesse signaled his departure for other activities, at least an adjournment to the front porch for studies, leaning against the railing, perhaps later adjourning to the rear of the property where a buggy ride might offer escape for both. The nonverbal communication was clear to Lou.

Soon after Sally's birth, Lou's requirements at work became less intense. With little effort on his part, Frank assumed more responsibility, accepting a small retainer from Lou, for Lou's sake, terming it a consulting fee. In reality, he appeared at L. J. Jensen's two or three times a week. Frank sensed more grudging approval from Joe, and he assured Lou that he had no designs on the business per se. Joe admitted to his brother that, "You know, I don't mind working with Frank, Lou, he keeps us on track, and he likes it when I call him counselor."

Closer to home, Jesse's behavior gave credibility to the idea that certain traits and proclivities might be inherited. Dora saw a sparkle in his eyes that Lou might have drawn out if he were home more often. He didn't often show a humorous side but one night as he grabbed a McGuffey Fourth Reader and, without opening it, quoted from memory "Lazy Ned" and "Try, Try Again," he and his mother both laughed, Dora hearing in the exchange something her brother Viv might have done. She missed her brother and was reminded of him anytime she caught a whiff of cigar smoke as she walked along Washington Avenue. He had been instrumental in steadying Lou's business at a critical time. She felt more than gratitude but feared that she and her brother would see less of each other in the future.

⌒

Frank and Annie had recently traveled to St. Louis to visit their ailing father. By the time they got there he was on the mend. Glad that their visit was a tonic nonetheless, Frank accompanied his sister on a shopping trip and, after spending some time with Crawford and his family, booked two sleeping compartments, going West. Returning, Frank had brought a special gift to Lou from his elder brother Crawford. In fact, it was one of two copies of *Ranch Life and the Hunting Trail* which had been given to Crawford by T. R. Roosevelt himself. With his typical modesty, Frank shared that he had been present at the time.

"Not exactly hot off the press, Lou, but Crawford thought you might enjoy it being a genuine Westerner and the only son of a pioneer my brother knows, through me."

Lou received it shaking his head, Frank assuming that, as Lou turned it over in his work worn hands, though not as well educated as himself, he had an appreciation for the unique offering.

In addition, Frank came with news of a superior business opportunity for Lou. A friend of Crawford's, Norton Russell Bagley, was involved in Colorado mining. Because of Frank's friendship with Lou and concern for the Jensens' future, he wanted to make a pitch for him to consider a new venture. If he thought the book would soften the deal, Frank was dead wrong.

As Frank paced the worn floor of Lou's office, he went on, after a fairly soft approach to his real subject.

"You are missing an opportunity that will really mean something. Instead of lumber it will involve machinery, metal equipment and supplies, along that line, Lou." Frank removed his coat and carefully placed it on the back of Lou's chair.

Lou at this point circled toward the front window. Frank was aware that a supposed glance up and down the street on Lou's part, masked a bit of time to answer with a forceful come-back.

Seizing the opportunity, Frank continued, "All kinds of freight will need to be moved and you," Frank punched the air with his finger, "are in a perfect locale to transfer products via your precious railroad." Frank nodded for emphasis, somewhat assured that he had made a compelling argument.

"I don't know, Frank, sounds risky, it's not my area." Lou shook his head and checked his watch which he drew from his vest pocket. Frank was struck by his friend's more measured response and he wondered how emphatic he could be as he pleaded his case.

At times Frank became weary of the speech about the seeking of lumber, buying it, felling it and he had an idea that Dora must feel that way also, though he refrained from invoking her name in the conversation. Lou shrugged his shoulders and Frank gritted his teeth.

"Lou, just take a look at one of these." He plopped down in Lou's chair. He had at the ready a copy of *The Lead and Zinc News:* "Ingersoll drills and Rand compressors, I think there's a future there, Lou. I know they have a rep staying at The Keeny House down on Wall Street." Frank gestured with his thumb. "Let me call him, it would be a start, either for investment or direct selling."

Lou stretched up to his full height. "But it's the railroad, Frank, that will make it all possible, road beds, standard and narrow. I know nothing about the machine lines you're talking about." Lou leaned against his desk, in Frank's view, stressing his position of firm command in his own store. Being somewhat taller than Frank, and folding his arms across his chest, Lou said, "I talk to a lot of people too, Frank, the ones out in the field. Lumber is key!" The finger jabbing the air was uncomfortably close to Frank's face.

Frank closed his eyes. He could only imagine how often Dora might have heard this spiel. "And then more lumber to build those very structures needed to support mining. Anyway, Frank, I'm committed north to Montana because of ma's property. It's an investment, too. Don't you see?"

Lou reached in back drawing a cigarette from the pack on his desk opened the day before. Lighting it, he squinted in the smoke. "Don't you see? I'm tied."

"Well, get untied, Lou." Frank rose from Lou's chair which sent it spinning on its wheels across the narrow room where it hit the wall and bounced away. "I'm telling you this is going to be the better investment and," he jabbed the air again with his finger, "it's in Colorado, close to home, closer than Montana. And by the way, Lou, you're not a kid, think of your family." He came close to invoking Dora's name but caught himself.

Lou stepped forward to clap Frank on the shoulder. He flicked his ashes to the floor without concern. Frank sensed that Lou wanted to yield.

"But now's not the time, can't swing it, Frank." Frank was more than ready and able to invest on Lou and Dora's behalf, but friendship dictated that he deferred to his friend's opinion as to not only his business but his family's needs.

The atmosphere, defused by Lou's gesture and infectious smile, progressed to an agreed-on need for a late lunch. The two men exited Lou's store, moving in an easy path toward the Saddle Rock Restaurant on 24th Street serving "Oysters in Every Style."

Chapter Nineteen
Uptown Celebration

The combination of anticipation, dust, sweat, and heat was made electric by the numerous eleven-year-old boys who scrambled everywhere for a spot to view the parade. They scuffed shoes, snagged clothing, and scratched arms as they climbed and shinnied up trees.

A shout of "Climb up here, Ben, it's better 'n over there!" reached Dora's ears. And Ben Coulter shouting back, "Yea, Francis, I got you beat now, don't you just wish you'd spied this limb first!" Both boys were friends of Jesse.

The Jensen party was comprised of Dora and Lou with Jesse, Darling, Sally, Delia and Mabel, whose ever ready arms held Sally. Since Jesse's birth, Mabel Stokes was thought of as not just Eliza's "hired girl," but a member of the family. She was on call at a moment's notice and having no family of her own, stayed next door with Eliza, having her own room, simply furnished, but tidy. Dora could see that Mabel's attention was trained on Oscar Guderson, a newly returned missionary for the

Church. Mabel waved to him and seemed anxious to show off her child-minding skills. A moment later, Lou took Sally from Mabel's arms and placed her in the Jensens' newly purchased baby carriage, leaving Mabel free to attempt a conversation with young Oscar.

The family had come to view the very best of any state's salute to the Fourth of July. The celebration had been honored in the Utah Territory since early pioneer days. Their next child would be their first one born in the State of Utah, that year, 1896, marking the long-sought achievement.

"Jess! Jess!" called Jesse's friends. Dora turned as far as she could, with the constraints of a new corset, to observe with pride her son's popularity as he threaded his way through the throng toward his schoolmates. She was not happy at the shortening of his name by the other boys, but as long as he answered to Jesse within the family circle, she could see no harm.

Even Lou was permissive about some of the new ways of young people. "Just so it doesn't get out of hand," he had said. "I'll know soon enough if we have to take strict measures."

Although it sounded authoritarian, Lou, as the head of the Jensen family, showed leniency toward their children. Dora looked at Lou with adoring eyes. He was just the sort of father their children needed, and they needed the stability of their father in Ogden, not some far away tract or field. For Dora, Ogden was home and as close to the Celestial Kingdom as she ever thought she'd come, at least without some serious rethinking on her part and behavior readjustment on Lou's. She didn't want to change her husband; and even with his vices—smoking and not attending priesthood meetings—his place at the head of the family was reflected in the vigor of their children. She liked their energy, and Lou encouraged it.

Dora squinted as she surveyed a few women close to her, carefully evaluating their hats, this focus due to her acquaintance with Annie Elgin. Lou encouraged her to take her glasses to public events, even if they remained on the delicate chain around her neck secured by a decorative breast pin. In fact, she often ignored this advice.

"I know you can hear me, Pol, but I also know you can't see," Lou had said before they left the house. "That's why you have the glasses from Dr. Rush. You can put them on and take them off as many times as you want, but at least take them." Dora simply glided down the hall away from him, to avoid further conversation.

Dora opened her parasol. Her hat had shaded her face and deflected the heat, but now she needed the additional shelter from the sun. She fanned herself slowly with her left hand. She enjoyed, as did Lou, the noisy hubbub of the occasion. The last few weeks Dora had suffered with the heat. She knew Lou would be delighted with another child, but for herself, the girls and Jesse were a perfect sized family. Still, she would be over thirty when her next baby was born, though Kibby Malan was three years older and expecting her fifth. Dora, however, had more help with household duties, thanks to Mabel, than some of her friends in the ward, who often teased her good naturedly about this good fortune.

❧

A week after the Fourth, Dora made her way to Annie Elgin's shop to see if anything less confining could be ordered by catalogue, now that her form was altered by her latest pregnancy. Previously Annie had put in an order for McKeones' Maize Flour Soap from Philadelphia and both women had been very pleased with the product. Dora's new corset bought from Mrs. Greenwell at ZCMI was clearly not going to take her through the summer into the fall. As soon as she got home from being out, she routinely shed it for a more forgiving chemise and wrapper.

Lou would soon notice her thickening waist, always the first sign for her. She had stopped nursing Sally months before and frankly did not miss the discomfort, different from when Darling was a baby.

As Dora waited for Annie to be free to talk, she admired the lavender suit which the milliner wore as she stepped gracefully from showcase to dressing table mirror, as she offered every enticement to her customers. Annie helped Clemmie Lloyd try on newly arrived straw hats. A small brimmed hat trimmed in violets completed Annie's outfit to further pique the interest of patrons, the object of this bringing orders for custom trimming with tulle, birds, and flowers to embellish basic styles.

Clemmie had told Dora as they met on 24th Street a week earlier, "Oh, Annie Elgin trimmed this for me last week. I think it's just the right amount of decoration.

Vibrant, but still subtle. I hope to pop in again soon, as she always has new offerings. Albert chides me for shopping too much, but he always pays the bills."

As soon as Annie was free, she and Dora settled for tea and small sandwiches at the back of the shop, rather than going to Blocks. Dora, candid about her pregnancy discomfort, found Annie a caring listener. After lunch, she looked through the catalogue with Dora and, after listening to her concerns, helped her make a selection. Annie ordered the undergarments by wire.

Dora always felt calmed by Annie's manner and although the two often shared slightly gossipy news, the friendship was a solid one. Dora often mentioned Frank's name, how helpful Annie's brother was to Lou in the store and what good friends they were.

Annie shared with Dora her opinion. "I'm sure Frank will return to St. Louis to find a wife and stay to join Crawford in his firm."

Dora felt a light reaction to the possibility that Frank wouldn't stay in Ogden, available with advice for Lou. On her own part, Dora enjoyed having him come to the house for tea or greeting him on the street as a friend. A smile from Frank, accompanied with an unmistakable look beyond mere social recognition, gave Dora a lift she couldn't deny. She saw no reason to share this evaluation with Lou, although she didn't assume Lou would feel any jealousy at all, Frank being his friend.

To reclaim the cool detachment Dora felt she needed to project after hearing this unwelcome news about Frank returning to St. Louis, she commented briefly on the newest decoration of support columns disguised by silk flowers and vines. On one counter, pairs of gloves were displayed on lacy table linens.

When Dora moved to leave, Annie gave a warm smile. "I'll call you as soon as your order arrives, Dora, and do pick up one of my new cards in the basket at the front. I've added a trellis motif which mimics what I use in the store. I aim to keep you coming back. But of course, more as a friend than a customer."

At this, the two women rushed forth for a friendly embrace.

Dora picked up one of Annie's cards and slipped it into a leather case in her satchel. On the card in delicate gilt script was written *Madeline Anne Elgin, Millinery, Trousseaux consultation a specialty.* Later, Dora would write Frank's name on the back of the card.

⌒

January 1898 saw the birth of Rennie at the home on 28th Street. Eliza pronounced the birth "easy as pie." Not to Dora, who had experienced the worst nausea of all her pregnancies and by early autumn had been forced to stay close to home, with the added discomfort of migraines several times a week. Yet, the delivery itself had been less arduous.

After the first six weeks, Dora's outlook improved. Her newborn was not particularly husky, but docile and easy. She felt grateful Lou was home, but she held her breath.

Lumber procurement still drew Lou north and, though extensive lectures on the future of lumber in furthering rail line access necessary for canal and dam construction had lessened, Dora knew his enthusiasm hadn't dimmed. He wanted to be at the forefront of building and development. In some respects, his dreams outpaced what was plausible, at least on the scale he envisioned.

Early in March, Eliza fell ill. Dora suggested to Lou that, to ease the household routine, Darling be sent up to Mound Fort for a short visit. Dora knew Darling would benefit from being with Dora's sister Nannie and her children and her mother, whom Darling saw infrequently. The next week, Lou set off with Darling, her favorite picture books packed in a small valise along with her clothes.

A week into Darling's visit, Lou wrote her a letter, which he read aloud to Dora for her approval:

Dear little Darling, mama sends you up a couple of clean aprons today by Uncle Joe. We hear that you are having a very nice time up there riding the donkey, and that you are a very good little girl. Now this pleases us very much and we want you always to mind what your grandma Barlow says to you and then she will like to have you with her. Our dear grandma here is very sick but we hope she will be better tomorrow. Doctor says he thinks she will be, and we want you to pray to God to make grandma well soon. When you want anything from here, ask Uncle Joe to tell papa what it is so we can get it for you. We miss you very much but as soon as grandma is better, we will have you come down. Jesse is quite a good boy now but would like to see his sister as would Sally and the baby. Mama sends her love and so we all do. Love, Papa.

The only change Dora suggested was to delete "very sick" and replace it with "ill," knowing the letter would be seen by her mother and sister. Dora had long ago been taught that "ill" was the preferred way to refer to less than perfect health.

Chapter Twenty
The Poplars

Lou returned with Darling and, at Dora's request, brought her mother. At their arrival, Dora and Eliza could see that Jane Dinah was very different from the woman they had seen at Christmas. The counsel Dora might have sought from her was no longer possible. Dora's mother stood, her arms folded across her chest as if she were listening for something, her tousled head turning from side to side. It was clear that Nannie had attempted to tame her unbound hair with various clips and pins, but the wiry strands squirmed out of the containment as she herself did, disengaging from Dora's attempts to embrace her. Dora saw her mother appeared to be hearing a message in the breeze or watching for a sign in the minute flutter of leaves.

She turned to Dora with a puzzled look. "When do we start? I have so wanted to go to Lagoon. Will we have enough food?"

At this display, Jesse and Sally stood in rapt attention. They had never heard their grandmother talk in this way. They both turned to Dora, but she hustled them out of the room before more was said.

Dora couldn't share any of the uncertainties she had relating to Lou's erratic travel schedule. In fact, he was traveling even then. Her concerns about his health were constant. Her mother could no longer lend an ear to her frustrations. Dora was grateful that at least Nannie would be at Mound Fort, several miles north of Ogden, where Dora had grown up in the Barlow family, before she had ever thought she would live more than a few porches away from her mother. Dora had relied less and less on her family there, not just because of the distance, but she and Lou had become closer to Eliza, and Dora had her ward sisterhood and Annie Elgin and her brother Frank were responsive and caring. But the desire on Dora's part to convey her love for her mother was still just as strong.

Dora clasped her mother in her arms. Jane Dinah yelped at the sudden show of affection and smiled in a way unfamiliar to Dora. Not the reassuring "all will be well" look, which used to give Dora confidence.

Soon Jane Dinah traveled the short distance to Mound Fort, accompanied by Lou, her son-in-law, where she would have the comfort of loved ones and familiar surroundings again, especially her daughter Nannie. Dora missed their conspiratorial youth, planning for their future, not that many years ago, really. Now only letters and phone conversations knitted the sisters together as they exchanged news often weeks out of date. A recent call from Nannie informed Dora that, "Oh, Dora dear, didn't I tell you about Jamie's fall? I can't imagine omitting that event. It was awful, I can tell you." At that point Dora realized that she had no idea who Jamie was or even his age, assuming that Jamie was a nickname for James Barlow, a new baby in the family named after a recently deceased family member.

Eliza had quarreled with Dora over many things, among them the fussiness relating to how furniture was arranged in a room, or even where items were placed on tables. Of more importance was her specific viewpoint regarding child-rearing. Eliza knew that Lou loved his wife dearly and, to be fair, Dora had produced three children; however, two of the three seemed not as robust as Eliza would have liked. She had noticed of late, in Darling, a peaked look. She was usually energetic and inquisitive, especially for a girl. Darling, nearly six, was put through her paces, performing barbell exercises which Eliza had designed to build up her chest muscles. At Eliza's insistence, these were performed outdoors. Also required was a brisk walk once a day toward the foothills and back, the degree of briskness and length determined by Eliza's inclination at the time. In a few weeks in fact, Eliza told Dora, without preamble, that she had planned to take Darling, Jesse and Sally on a two-week excursion to the farm she had purchased in Montana. In truth she had discussed such plans in Dora's hearing a year before, but illness or weather had always delayed a trip. Both Lou and Dora had agreed that Eliza was, for the most part, a positive influence and their only active grandparent. There was no doubt in Eliza's mind that her youngsters had willing minds, especially Jesse, soon to have his eighth birthday. And the land described by Eliza, enhanced by a rustic house, had been bought as an investment with Eliza's sister and brother-in-law. It was situated between Bozeman and Anaconda.

"Best thing in the world for them," Eliza announced one evening at dinner, tapping her hand in a staccato beat as she spoke. "Why, we can walk from where the train stops at Two Dot, just a short distance to the farm road," she beamed. This from a woman who admittedly had come to the Salt Lake Valley with a handcart company and recently had battled pleurisy, which attacked her system on a yearly basis. She warmed to her subject; dark eyes flashing, she looked pointedly at Lou who smiled at the dim recollection of his mother's sister and her husband, though glancing at Dora, Eliza knew that Dora had not met the couple. "Well, anyway, they will meet us with the wagon as we are on our way, and carry us and our baggage the rest of the way. What do you think?" Her head bobbed with enthusiasm as she in turn looked around at those at the table.

During this presentation Dora was mute. She waited for a more private time alone with her husband. She had no intention of permitting such a journey. Thankfully, there had been no talk of how Eliza would manage traveling with a baby, still nursing. Dora refrained from injecting this thought into the conversation. Her own presence on the jaunt had not been referenced. She would withhold permission for this excursion.

᠗

Dora was content for the most part. Her home was as she wanted. Next spring, the path leading up to the front door, as well as the side entrance where friends called, would be fragrant with lilac. She planned to fill in the empty spaces with smaller plants. She told Lou she wouldn't mind scooting along on a small pillow to save her knees, digging and trimming as she progressed. She would carefully clip any withering stems from her bedding plants. Recently marigolds joined the asters and mums she had chosen.

Dora looked around the room, pleased that Jesse was at his books and Sally worked on a scrap book with Darling, who excelled in the details of cutting and pasting. Sally provided the wispy, though legible, descriptive text as dictated by Darling. Earlier the two had put the baby to bed, humming to lull him and tiptoeing out as they had seen their mother do, though she would transfer him to her own bed to nurse him if he awoke during the night.

Lou's feet were propped up on a stool close to the fire. He had smoked a cigarette carefully putting aside the Honey Dew coupon he saved up for books. Dora looked at the coupon he handed her for her inspection.

"Only twenty-five to send in and they send me a free book."

Dora turned the paper to the underside where he had carefully printed the names of his three choices: *Camille*, *King Solomon's Mines* and *Ivan The Serf*. Crossed out were *A Crown of Shame* and *The Other Man's Wife*.

Dora was not impressed. Her eyebrows raised as she mouthed the titles.

He began peeling an orange taken from a bowl on the lamp table between their chairs. Dora had told him not to bother with this method of reducing the smell of tobacco on his fingers, since smelling like an orange peel was almost as bad. At least he didn't chew and for that she was most grateful.

Soon after the girls had gone off to bed and Jesse still studied in a small alcove near his bedroom, the couple had some time to themselves. Lou again lit a cigarette. He held out the package to Dora and she, taking him by surprise, took one. He lit it for her, and Dora smoked her first cigarette without so much as a cough.

∾

Lou announced the next morning that he would make another trip to Montana.

This news was unwelcome and somewhat unexpected. Dora felt the fingers of depression grip her. The wool shrug she wrapped around her shoulders would not provide the warmth of encircling arms or the security of an embrace or the possibility of leaning hard on an immovable chest. This was missing. Bedtime, after a wearisome day without Lou, was welcome. She allowed the dog to lie across her feet, the comforting sounds of his sighs as he settled in, a substitute for human presence.

After his departure, Dora sat and rocked in front of the cold fire grate. Lou was inspecting the Montana property on the Madison River. He was due back within the next three weeks but would be camping and unreachable until he returned to Butte. Dora didn't often contact him when he was away, although phone in an emergency was available in some established camps. Often Lou ran the telephone wires himself just for that purpose, ingeniously using a combination of bare tree trunks and improvised supports secured to the sides of temporary buildings.

Dora had words with Eliza one afternoon after an unusually substantial meal which Eliza had pronounced heavy, but one she had eaten with gusto. Dora expressed her concern about Rennie, who was teething.

Eliza, in answer to a comment from Dora about his growth, had said, "Dora, you baby him too much and what kind of a name is Rennie anyway? I thought Lou was set on David Kay."

Named for a friend of Lou's from Philadelphia whom he had met at West Point, Dora thought the name a mark of sophistication. She held back her comment and instead said, "In the first place, Rennie is in fact his name, and I'm still nursing, and I don't think he seems as sturdy as I would like." There she got it out but got no more from Eliza.

The baby was particularly adorable, his fist grasping onto her little finger. Still, she saw he was not as vibrant as the others had been at the same age.

◦⌇

A few days later, receiving a message from an orderly at The Poplars, Eliza set off on Jackson, her brown mare. Lines were down because of a brisk wind signaling a storm's approach, and the smell of snow was in the air. Instead of a phone call, the usual method for transmitting emergency information, a young man had ridden from The Poplars to ask for her services.

As Eliza rode, she thought about the impending delivery of Maud Barnes, for that was the message the young man carried. Maud was a thirty-four-year-old mother of six whom Eliza had befriended after she had reached the Utah Territory. Eliza was sure her friend was carrying twins, maybe triplets.

As she explained briefly to Dora, her last delivery of that number had been when she herself was pregnant with Lou and crossing the plains. Eliza was called to aid in the delivery of a young widow with a four-year-old girl. All three of the babies were stillborn, and Eliza was put in charge of the surviving little girl for the remainder of the journey. The mother, able to rest the remainder of the trek, had arrived in the Salt Lake Valley in somewhat restored health. Thereafter she talked often of how Eliza had helped in time of need.

The two women remained friends and often met when Eliza was in Salt Lake. Maud was the third woman to bond with the other two, having experienced similar lessons learned on the trail, as well as difficult conditions after she reached the Utah Territory. Since her husband was ill, care of her other children had been given over to another family in their ward.

The Poplars was initially built to fill an urgent need for medical care north of Salt Lake. A previous hospital, close to the Jensen home, only survived a year. Whether a victim of the economic slump or not, it did not survive, reflecting also the fate of potential patients who sought help from the medical community in Ogden. Obstetrical care was primarily home based; Ogden physicians preferred having the advantage of the wider range of care which Salt Lake offered. An emerging need seen by Eliza, at first without much support, was for the care of orphans. Placement in the community, where citizens already had financial difficulties, was resisted. Friends of Eliza, many from the medical community, saw her effort as wholesome in every respect. Often, girls in trouble would come seeking a place to stay until they delivered. Ideally, a member of their extended family would accept the girls in temporary shelter and then give a home to the infant. In rare cases, formal adoptions were arranged.

The Poplars welcomed the girls, who were often as young as fourteen, thanks to Eliza. These young, prospective mothers were given light chores, mainly to keep them busy and allow them to work together as a family might. They were asked to help in the kitchen and, if they wished, could help mind babies and young children, who as yet had not been placed elsewhere. Eliza made sure books and writing materials were available for the girls, since they could no longer go to school. A clean warm dormitory provided them with a sense of community.

On 28th Street, Rennie and Darling were feverish and restless. Dora was no stranger to illness, but she knew better than to take any of the medicines in Eliza's cabinet without knowing what she was treating. She had heard often enough the counsel to "purge 'em, puke 'em, sweat 'em," but she didn't normally ascribe to this adage and felt it was an overly simplistic approach to symptoms. She even knew Eliza no longer ascribed to it.

Later in the evening, Dora awakened Sally and roused Jesse from his reading at the table and told them that she was going to take Darling and Rennie to The Poplars so their grandmother could see to them.

Dora didn't wish to present a picture of alarm but with her hair braided as usual for bedtime, she saw Jesse's face register disbelief that his mother would leave the house without attending more to her appearance.

Dora asked Sally, now in her dressing gown, to heat up the morning's leftover coffee, then go next door to summon Delia and Mabel. She sent Jesse to the barn to ready horse and wagon.

Dora pulled on a pair of Lou's heavy pants and remembered the night Eliza had done the same in a very different situation. Jesse was just a baby then. The garment had been destined for a future cutting for rag rug strips or for one of Eliza's crazy quilts. "And, they *are* crazy-looking, Lou." Dora had once blurted out this opinion barely out of earshot of her mother-in-law. She buttoned the pants, cinched in the waist with a belt and stuffed the too-long trouser legs into her boot tops. Lou had insisted on the purchase of these practical boots, saying that even on a picnic in the foothills, they were more practical than Dora's dainty high tops. She was glad now she had them and pulled on two pairs of stockings besides.

Outside the wind was whipping the lilac bushes about the porch. Light snow swirled next to the house in top-like patterns, squealing like Rennie's toy train whistle. The lilacs, prematurely budding, were full of promise; and after a warm spell, spring seemed within reach. Lou always brought in the first twig showing buds, even then emitting the evocative fragrance. But March storms were treacherous.

As Dora bundled the two strangely quiet children into the wagon in down padded bolsters, she added wrappers of oiled cloth as a further protection. She gritted her teeth at the insensitivity of her mother-in-law, who seemed to put her patient's welfare before her family. Though in truth, Dora knew this wasn't fair. But she was resentful toward Lou, in Montana now when she desperately needed him.

"Dr. God" is what she called Eliza under her breath. At first she had offered "Mother Jensen" but had been put off by Eliza's response: "I'm not your mother!" So, she settled on Mrs. Jensen. Lou said she took Eliza's comments much too seriously. Whatever she was called, Eliza had left Rennie and Darling to nurse a bad girl.

This was, in fact, an incorrect assumption but it fueled another conflict with her mother-in-law—Dora's assumption that Eliza only helped girls in trouble. These thoughts ebbed as she climbed aboard the wagon and as she gulped down a mug of creamy lukewarm coffee offered by Sally. She told Jesse and Sally to stay inside until Delia could dress and come to see after them. She then waved as Delia approached. A few cursory directions and she was off.

Dora drove slowly north, her thoughts turning to Lou and the two warring viewpoints: how well he provided for her, yet she considered him uncaring for not being with her now. However, the responsibility of the drive as the snow and wind increased became uppermost in her mind. The reliable horse had no trouble pulling the three since Eliza's horses were used to a much heavier load. As the reins slid across her palms, she thought about a long-ago note from Lou:

Dora, a crowd of us is going out in the large bobsleigh this evening, and I should be pleased to have your company so . . . If you choose to go, I will call at about seven o'clock pm, yours, Lou.

That was just three years before they married, before he went to West Point. That decision had been Eliza's,

Dora was sure of it. He had told Dora he was only thinking of her and their future, starting off in a marriage with
some financial certainty.

"But what about the store?" she had asked him. She
knew he loved the business, the rough and tumble of visiting townspeople as they traded.

Lou's letters from New York had conveyed his enthusiasm to her once he settled in. Dora's were not as faithfully sent. The photograph of him taken in his West
Point uniform had fairly burned her eyes as she stared at
it propped on her writing table. But soon enough he was
home and hers, and now still the same. Dora heard more
than once from Eliza that she had been disappointed in
her son's decision to leave West Point early.

Darling, just turned six and doing so well in school,
was whimpering. This was very uncharacteristic. Darling was known to endure skinned knees without even
noticing, reacting with giggles as her mother tried to
clean miniscule dirt specks from her skin. Rennie was
quiet. Dora looked over her shoulder at the two. "Snug
as a bug in a rug," Darling said with a weak little smile
as if to answer the question in Dora's eyes. The child's
burnished cheeks looked as if they would burst.

"We'll be there in three shakes of a dead sheep's tail,"
Dora said, but Darling didn't react or even smile. Dora
was sure that Darling, intelligent though she was, had
failed to grasp the idiotic meaning of the saying parroted
by Eliza, but at least she usually giggled in response.

"Your grandmother will make you better, and tomorrow when we're home again, Mama will make cold

custard to drink, creamy for you to swallow. You can have all you want, and Uncle Joe will bring our supplies, and I'll have all the eggs and sweet milk I need and extra vanilla. That's what you like, isn't it, Darling?" Dora winked at her sweet girl, a skill they had perfected as a game, winking back and forth multiple times.

Dora's scratchy voice rendered her attempts at conversation meaningless. The snow had been light as they started out, but so much had fallen in the last hour, it added to previous drifts. She didn't look forward to the drive back. *If* Eliza returned with her, if only, that was her wish. Now she needed the steely strength and resolve of Eliza and even Jane Dinah in her earlier years.

Not a sound came from her tiny passengers, although Dora kept up a steady monologue about what they would do next week, next summer, how grown up papa would find them and Darling would surprise papa with her paper weaving workbook, and indeed it was so very precise.

Dora, finally exhausted from talking into the wind, her throat raw, concentrated on the horse's flanks. Her arms were stiff from the unaccustomed pull and jerk of driving. Dora was tired and cold, not wrapped as warmly as the children, and she was frightened. Ahead was a stand of poplars and cottonwoods. She knew she was very close now. In a moment the lights of The Poplars were visible.

Now that she had arrived, dread rose within her; relief, but fear even more. Just seeing Eliza and answering her questions as to why she would bring the children out on such a night would be intimidating. But in the transference of Rennie and Darling to waiting arms, selfish worries and thoughts in Dora's mind which framed her own feelings rather than the pitiful need at hand, faded completely. At least until she alighted and numbly walked into the bright corridor.

Eliza was alarmed to see Dora's state. She had both children put in a well-lit room where she could examine them. She unwrapped her two grandchildren to assess their condition. Eliza took Rennie's hand in her own. "This child has scarlet fever," she said. "Darling too, I'm afraid."

Dora's face twisted beyond recognition. "But that can't be! Eliza, they are safe at home, and the others will be and . . ."

Eliza interrupted her. "There are cases in the valley, only one up here but, Dora, I can't be mistaken here. I don't think our little one will live through the night."

Dora cried out, "Surely they will come through this!"

Eliza slowly shook her head and moved to put her arms around her daughter-in-law, who looked now from Rennie to Darling as if they might dissolve before her eyes. Then Dora sank in Eliza's arms. Eliza carried her to a low bed in the same room. While Dora slept, Eliza, and others in her employ, worked with the children.

In the morning, Rennie was gone. The next day, Darling seemed improved, but Eliza was not optimistic. Word was sent to Delia. She was brought to The Poplars to ride back with Dora and Darling. Since the storm was over, the ride home would be a faster one. Eliza would follow behind them in another wagon with a small casket.

As Dora headed home, Delia at the reins, the comfort of what life had been, was put away like winter clothing in the spring. They had Jesse, Sally and Darling but their baby was gone. Lou had not even begun to know this son, just over a year old, so mild and agreeable. Indeed, after an arduous pregnancy, Dora had found Rennie's temperament easy.

Her breasts ached with a familiar twinge, a painful reminder to feed her son. She would bind her chest, though the ache would continue. Milk soaked the cotton vest under her shirtwaist. She sobbed, hating the process and herself even more. Darling, her sweet girl, lay still in the place Eliza had prepared for her in the back. Dora felt ashamed to consider her own discomfort at all. She resigned herself to exhaustion, leaning against Delia who drove on toward 28th Street.

Lou reached Ogden the next morning. His mother had telephoned him, sparing him the shock of delayed news, telling him of Rennie's death from scarlet fever. Within a few hours of Lou's return, six-year-old Darling had died as well.

Dora and Lou stared at Darling's body on the bed. She lay beneath a sheet, embroidered by Eliza with tiny roses. Lou noticed the contrast in color as its fold reached Darling's pale chin, but he made no comment. Lou was unable to detect any reaction from Dora. He ached to hold her and have her hold him. Her physical rigidity, so unlike her, frightened him. Her hands remained folded in her lap; Lou supposed they were cold and stiff.

His mother had seen this reaction many times in her work. The instinctive inner cry for what is most needed and desired, is denied by a greater need to remain disengaged, a way of guarding against additional hurt. Not surprised to see Dora turn away from Lou, Eliza urged her son to respect this initial response. A change would come in time, and if he showed patience now, their marriage would strengthen, as the loss they shared eventually softened.

Under Eliza's direction, Delia and Mabel kept to the parlor, readying it for whenever the service would be held. They also provided food and coffee. Eliza and Lou shared a small brandy. Dora shook her head at the offer.

ᴐ—

Eliza left the room to the couple and their daughter. She had been quick to diagnose and yet not soon enough and, in the end, powerless to intervene. She had felt sure Darling would survive. She had been wrong. She had seen much in her forty-eight years, but losing two grandchildren in less than twenty-four hours was beyond any medical preparation she had received. The babies lost on her trek west were tragic, as she had become friends with their mothers. And being pregnant herself, all the more, she was drawn to the precipitous event of bringing life into the world. But Eliza had never lost one from her own body. The objectivity of delivering deformed babies, or those birthed before their time, all was in her experience, but this loss of two so dear to herself, to her boy, to Lou and Dora was unique.

She went to her house next door, usually empty of children's voices. For that sound, she only had to step, just a few steps, so close together were the houses. Where her son and his family lived, a baby's cry and the unintelligible vocal patterns of toddlers were dear to her. Darling had been a conversational child. The two on their walks together, joyfully examined whatever caught their attention. Eliza had seen such curiosity in Darling and, coupled with a pleasing disposition, this first granddaughter was a worthy balance to Jesse, who was also bright but often withdrawn.

Eliza had delivered Rennie just over a year before, and six years before that, Darling. She had held them first, even before their mother and, in turn, had presented them to her son. Her hands could recall the feel and weight of each, even six years apart. Their first look at the world had been guided by her.

❧

Lou had asked good friend John Edward Carver to perform the ceremony for his infant son Rennie and six-year-old Darling. The Jensen parlor was transformed by banks of flowers and greens into what seemed like a heavenly bower evoking joy, as requested by Lou. He understood that Dora was in shock and could not abide a morbid farewell.

Dora Vivian, always called Darling, and Rennie were buried in the Ogden City Cemetery. The creamy white stone marked both children as they were laid to rest side by side. Chosen by Lou, the stone featured a simple floral decoration above their names. His friend, John Bott from Brigham City, did the work for the Jensen family.

After the interment, the temperature warmed. Lou and Dora, sitting side by side, remained long after all had gone back to the Jensen home for a meal prepared and served by the women of the ward.

Joe and Eliza waited in the funeral carriage to drive the couple home. There were no words between them, only their joined hands; the warmth ineffectual, but a hint of the history between them. The persistent chattering of birds in a leafless shrub was the only sound. At last Lou rose, offering his hand to Dora.

Joe quickly jumped down from the carriage to settle his brother and Dora and drive them home.

⌒

Frank, who was in St. Louis, heard from his friend about the children's deaths. He sent a floral tribute, then left with Annie for Ogden at the earliest opportunity. He resolved to exert all his energy to aid his friend in any way. Frank could lift the burden of the store. If that would release Lou to spend more time comforting Dora and his children, Frank would not count the cost.

Memorial for Dora Vivian Jensen

It is with profound regret that the kindergartners of Ogden will notice the death of little Vivian Jensen. For three years she has been a faithful worker in their little band and who graduated in this year from my class. At the closing exercises none were more veracious than she and none entered into the spirit of the closing exercises with a keener sense of appreciation and joy. Now alas, she is called to the home of her master and we are sorely grieved over the loss of this dear angelic child. Our heart responds in sympathy to those of the grief-stricken parents. May the spirit of Him who said, "Suffer the little children to come unto me . . . for of such is the kingdom of heaven," be their comfort and inspiration in this their hour of dark despair. Vernice Monson

Photographs

Ogden, Utah, Wasatch Mountains

Lou as a newly married young business man.

Eliza with Lou
1868 after arrival in Utah.

Lou
West Point Class of 1893

Eliza
Later Years

Dora—age 15

Blue Chest

Part Three
Letters from Montana

Chapter Twenty-One
Ogden

In 1899, Dora received by courier from the court—at least he identified himself that way—a summons on legal form and witnessed by her own brother Viv Barlow and a friend of Lou's, a court reporter where Lou served as clerk.

The District Court of the 2nd Judicial District of the State of Utah, named Lou as plaintiff and Dora as defendant. It was in fact a summons for her to appear within twenty days, "failure to do so, judgement will be rendered." It was signed by Lou as plaintiff as well as attorney.

The particulars were set forth in legal formality:

1. *Their address on 28th Street identifying each by name and relationship, further stating that, "the defendant has ever been to this plaintiff a true and dutiful wife."*

2. *The plaintiff can conjure up no malfeasance or nonfeasance in her official capacity as such.*

3. *That there are two children, now living as the issue of said marriage to wit Jesse and Jane Ellen, known to all as Sally, both in the eyes of their parents, perfect in every respect.*

4. *That this plaintiff does not know a good thing when he has it and cannot endure the devotions and happiness of as intelligent a wife and therefore prays the court.*

5. *That should he ever ask or pray (which he rarely does) the court to dissolve the bonds of matrimony, now and hereafter existing between the plaintiff and defendant that the court will at once order an investigation conducted under the auspices of a competent physician to determine his fitness for consignment to that state institution in Provo, Utah, that should he pray for the custody of the two minors herein mentioned and rob them of their adorable mother's intelligent and noble training, may he be a hiss among men hereafter.*

This pretend summons brought tears to Dora's eyes. How like Lou to use all the vocabulary he had picked up to bring a smile to his wife's face. There was no doubt in Dora's mind that her husband adored her and would have given his life to spare her the pain she had suffered.

Morgan Utah 12/13/1899

My dear Pol, how are you getting along my darling? The weather here is much milder than last

*week. Monday I made a tour in the cutter and
yesterday I was out to Porterville about six miles
away. I visited several people and the reason for
my visit I put before them in the best positive manner but with the same result. My labor stirs them
up and I get lots of promises to come down before
the holidays but although two of them came down
yesterday and paid $ 85.00 into the agent's office,
there wasn't more promised. There is another
man here, who on my efforts really has had some
additional money paid in, and I have had several
inquiries for merchandise and another rep writes
that they are well satisfied with my efforts as my
reports are specific and truthful. So, I guess I'm
doing all right. Anyway, I will send Frank Elgin
a letter covering Santa Claus and other matters.
I think I will get away about Friday, so after that
you will write me up at Coalville. Lovingly, Lou.*

The letterhead was elaborate and impressive: Co-
operative Wagon and Machine Co., dealing in imple-
ments in Utah and Idaho. On the director's list were
Heber J. Grant and George Q. Cannon, prominent leaders in the Mormon church.

However, this was the latest point of contention
between Lou and Dora. Not that Lou had erred in link-
ing, even temporarily, with another company of impeccable reputation, but that Dora read it as more movement
away from his Ogden location . . . which it was.

As the first few months of the new year, 1900, sped by,

economic matters resulting from his being away from the store arose. His contention and comment that lumber had to be logged and that "it doesn't just slide into the racks without toil," took their confrontations to a new level and rose to a degree neither could deny.

In March of the new year, as Lou returned to Ogden after additional buying of timber tracts in more remote areas, for a few weeks it turned out, the couple faced each other after a hearty lunch of left-over pork roast and potatoes.

"Lou, why have you taken on what, I can only see as part time work with this new company, cooperative wagon or whatever, when you have your own business with an office right on Washington with Joe and now Frank to help and other workers for the lumber yards? I just don't understand it."

Lou laid his fork and knife on his plate making sure it would not drip on the cloth to upset his wife further.

"Dora, you have to look beyond today. The lumber supply will lead to rail construction and of course will lead to more travel, but we will be better for it. You saw how I decided to concentrate on lumber and drop the wholesale grocery inventory, though it was for a time profitable. Now I'm further pushing everything away except," and here he jabbed his finger very close to her nose, "except if it supports the railroad future construction goals. Don't you see? The little work, but important work, I do with a company that furthers the goal of growth in the area, I'm knocking myself out to push." He sat back in his chair seemingly worn out with the effort of convincing Dora that he knew what he was doing. "I've got to eventually distance myself completely from the grocery and grain area. It's called consolidation. We may not have prosperity, but if I can help it, we will have financial ease in the future. Remember when I assured you in '93, when it was bad for a lot of people, that folks had to eat, and then things would get better and building would pick up again?" Lou tapped energetically on the table, "Well, that happened, we were able to feed people and building did come along and you know as well as I do that the railroads are key."

Dora wasn't at all sure that the railroads were key. Railroad growth had certainly played old harry with her life, she knew that much. Dora fought the urge to shake her head. She stood, feeling that Lou was patronizing her, and feeling a need to move about, actually encircling Lou as he sat. She picked up a bowl and pivoted toward the kitchen, then turned plunking the bowl back on the table loudly, saying, "What you don't grasp, Lou,"—a note of exasperation crept into her voice—"is that every time you jump to something else, there is a financial cost as you change stock or even lose the grocery and grain business you've had for years. It looks like, to others I'm sure, that you can't settle on anything."

Dora sat herself down across from Lou. "Joe may not be a dynamo, but he's your brother and works as hard as he is able to keep things going when you travel. And of course Frank is a great help."

Lou stood, and turned from Dora who saw that her comments had found their mark.

He didn't know what to say. He felt weak and, in the face of her exhortation, unprepared to rebut anything she had said. He felt the sting of tears and knew if he turned to her now, they would both dissolve into even more of an emotional scene wherein each would apologize, Lou would regain some stature as head of his family and she, for the moment, would relinquish the pedestal of forthrightness she had claimed.

He half turned toward Dora, his expression stern. "I'll be in the store until supper, Dora." He then exited from the house, retrieving his coat and hat, stamping about for emphasis on the porch.

As an early spring enveloped all in the possibility of being outdoors more, Dora's children with friends and she herself blooming with the lilacs Lou had planted, he again took to the road. His letters, coming soon after he left, were tender. He was not insensitive to Dora's burdens at home. If a string of Lou's letters failed to mention this, he instead highlighted his efforts to find ways to add to his family's comfort financially. Dora tried to see this viewpoint. Her love for Lou had matured and changed in ways she would not have expected, but she missed their actual closeness, the good natured back and forth, the jokes they shared, even reading aloud to each other; all that had somehow dimmed, because it wasn't true, it didn't exist. Other, that is, than what he committed to paper, the words and phrases which so identified Lou, on paper, and she wanted his real self again.

The pretend summons, months before, had the desired effect; it drew her toward Lou, his charm, humor and creativity, attributes he had used years before and even now, to win her. But the mention of two surviving children she had found jarring. Rennie and Darling's existence had been erased. Dora brooded over memories which still had the power to hurt. She sought to harness her energy for the positive goals she and Lou had tried to work through, but their current unraveling of plans, and divergent opinions, made for thin ice encounters, one comment often stopping further conversation altogether. The couple's inability to decide how to be of one mind, strained the marital bond.

The letter, written weeks before the previous Christmas, still had the power to cause her pain. Though Dora had provided for the children's Christmas in a small way, wrapping many small inexpensive gifts in colorful paper, she knew that what they wanted for Christmas was to see their father. Morgan might as well have been St. Louis. The particulars that she should write him at Coalville, put the lid on an unwelcome Christmas surprise for her by assuring that, he may not get to Ogden at all. And that indeed came to pass. The family celebrated Christmas without Lou, Lou being delayed because of a blizzard. This did not surprise Dora, or Eliza. Providing money through Frank for "Santa Claus," his way of easing finances for her, in her mind placed an undue burden on his friend. It was not Frank's place to enable her to provide financially for her children.

If the children missed Lou, Dora's need paralyzed her. She had lacked her usual enthusiasm to bake for the holidays. She prepared in the kitchen alone, without Lou's sweet kisses on her neck as she prepared dough or stirred cooking sherry into the delectable sauce on the stove. She imagined how she would feel if their separation were permanent. In desperation she called Annie, who insisted on Dora meeting her the following day at her millinery.

"Come in, Dora." As Dora walked toward Annie's welcoming smile, shiny brass tacks spaced along the long counter-top blinked at her. She passed fabric and trim to be measured, items which would have usually had her full interest.

Noticing Dora's downcast expression, Annie said, "I know you have no interest in a hat today, dear." Annie offered a cup of tea and a plate of shortbread but Dora gave such a tortured look that Annie didn't insist.

"Annie, I'm not a newly married girl. I try to keep my own counsel and I can figure things out pretty well so I'll just say what I think, and you can tell me how it sounds or am I either mad or selfish?"

"Go on, Dora." Annie motioned for her friend to have a seat.

"I haven't told this to a living soul but I sense I can unburden myself to you. I don't know why exactly." She hesitated only a moment, sensing that in Annie she had a trusted listener. "I know Lou wouldn't have changed a thing these years since we've been married, even with the pain we've suffered, but—"

Annie didn't urge her further, waiting.

"He is so smart, Annie, look at what he does with figures, with the business, and yet he washed out of math of all things at West Point and but for that, he could have had a career in the Army, although he never talked of a military life. I know his mother urged him."

"But he came back home and married you and started a family, and lucky a man is he, Dora," Annie said.

Dora reached for the shortbread and Annie poured the tea.

"He knows that Frank and all his other friends have better educations but when he travels, he's not so much with people who have been back East to school. The people he deals with in a practical way know he's reliable and his honesty has never been questioned."

Now Annie turned her head to one side and caught Dora in her gaze. "Well, that's the important thing then, isn't it? What kind of a man he is, not what he hasn't been exposed to." She gestured with a sweep of her hand. "There's time for that later. Whatever he puts his mind to, he will master it, I'm sure of it."

"You are sweet to say that, Annie. I know he is trying to make good, make his mark as he says. He sees into the future, he really does. He knows how important the railroads will be to get things done."

"You sound like Lou, now, although I don't know him as well as Frank does, of course."

Dora laughed. "I've heard his ideas so much, and I do believe in them. I just wish this progress didn't come at such a cost for all of us. He's a respected businessman, it's just that he's not here to appreciate it and take his place as a community leader. Frank liked him from the start, and I'm pleased that they are lodge brothers."

Annie waited a moment, taking a sip of her tea before replying. "Maybe what you see for him is no longer what he wants, Dora. Maybe he's more fulfilled out on the road felling trees, so to speak, and surveying land. You know, being out in the open, but I know it's hard for you."

Annie rose, squared her shoulders, and walked around with a quick glance to the front of her store. All was in order. She saw that her helpers were dutifully noting new inventory, setting aside small cards of lace trim on the counter. She circled back around the settee.

"Lou, I'm told, has the respect not only of Frank but Burton French as well, and others like Dr. Carver, the Presbyterian minister. He's welcome in the fly fishing group at Burton's place in the canyon; on an island, Frank says, though I've never been there. But, you know, after what Lou does out in the field, those pursuits might be a bit tame, do you think?" Annie lightly tapped her pursed lips with a finger.

"But our marriage is suffering. What can I do, Annie?"

She sat down next to Dora patting her hand. "Let him lead, follow as I know you can. I wish I could offer better advice but as a maiden lady . . ." Annie said. "Although I have had a sweetheart, it is different in a marriage. I pray for you both for safety and special times together and for the children. We can talk often, anytime you need shortbread with your tea." Annie smiled at Dora and gave an encouraging nod.

Dora rose somewhat energized. As she left the shop, she stepped smartly to get her trolley. It did help to get out.

～

Months later, Dora's resolve had weakened. After a rather hasty return to Ogden, the first in the new year, Lou left again, vowing, as he usually did, that he would be gone a shorter time, this time. Dora chose to build on the positive aspects of time with the children, smarting nevertheless at the cool interaction with Lou, who tried to catch up with his business, at times showing little interest, so Frank told her, as he sat at his desk in the store, reviewing current sales and order updates.

Jesse, just turned nine, was an independent child, on his own when not in school, reading about science and archeology and flying. Six-year-old Sally needed playmates and benefitted from being with other children in the ward. Dora's friend, Kibby Malan, often brought her sons who were a little older and watchful when Sally was in the yard. Her cousin, Bess Wheelright, was newly married, with a baby on the way, and came to round out the group. Dora shared her the side yard with a table and chairs for a picnic area. The others brought sandwiches and Dora always had fruit. The group chose the name East Ogden Ladies Picnic and Child Betterment Society. All in fun, not shirking home or church duties, the young women could be free in conversation and, under watchful eyes, their little ones thrived. As their children played, their mothers shared plans and ideas for birthday gifts for the children, as well as surprise gifts and handwork keepsakes which they would give to their husbands. Dora looked forward to an early spring to renew the friendships she craved.

Chapter Twenty-Two
Travel North

Dear Dora, I wish you were here by my side as I write from camp. If I could arrange it, we would move up here permanently.

Dora knew Lou wanted her, figuratively at least, right along up behind him in the saddle, pursuing his new ideas and adventures. She shook her head. She stood at their dining room table, a cloth partially drawn aside as she had laid scalloped note paper to respond to this letter. Often the letters were her choice as well as Lou's for sharing ideas, a better choice than phone calls.

It's a dream, thought Dora. We can't just lock up and move the whole family.

She sat down as she continued reading. *I'm riding over each square mile of mother's property and it looks good. The scenery is breathtaking. Her land, halfway between Butte and Anaconda, is watered by the Madison River which runs through it. Anaconda is west of Butte. Go to the library which you know so well, and look up Montana. Anaconda is only nine miles from the continental divide!*

The land must be beautiful but what about leaving everything: friends, Ogden, their house? Dora felt pride in her community every time a new business or bank opened. She felt part of the downtown rush as shop owners recognized her, or as she met with friends at Blocks. Getting out more had caused her to pay more attention to her appearance, certainly fueled by association with Annie.

Lou's letter continued, and as she read, she tried to immerse herself in his enthusiasm.

I know you and mother haven't been close but that could change. Without missing a beat, Lou jumped to something that he knew she might find intriguing.

Back in '96, Bob Smith, when he was the governor, proposed an eight hour work day. Can you beat it? I'm telling you, dear heart, it's an exciting place to be. Mining is the electricity in the air, especially because of the copper potential, and how one hundred thousand workers will be needed. Of course, they can't do that without railroads!

Well, I know I'd better calm down. We have our home, don't we? But let's think about the future. Maybe I'll come up in a few months again for another look-see. Love to my babies, you and that sweet Sally girl and that serious little man. I'll try to be home in less than a week. But first, I'll spend a day or two in Butte just to listen to the talk on the street, you know. The Montana Register is a pretty decent paper, though not as fine as our Standard, but I'll bring a copy for you. As always, your devoted Lou. P.S, must get some sleep, was in the saddle most of the day, on and off, ha.

Dora took no real comfort in the words she read. He maintained that he was only thinking about a move,

and Dora sensed the humor was to cushion his growing desire to do just that. She certainly couldn't imagine
Eliza desiring a move north. Yes, she bought the land
but as more of an investment. After all, Eliza's life was
in Ogden. Dora walked around the room re-reading the
last paragraph to herself, then let the paper flutter to the
floor as she left the room to prepare for bed.

Conrad Montana, February 2, 1904

Dear Pol, I am almost to the Canadian border but
the way the trains run and make connections, I am
unable to say when we will reach there. We got
into Butte yesterday evening at six and left there
last night at 8. We went to Great Falls arriving at
2 am when we had to get out of bed and sit up until
9 am with weather 14 below. We reached Lether-
idge Canada at 11 pm and then had to take another
train for Mc Leod, due to arrive at 1:30, then we
lay there until 3 pm the next day, and arrived some
time during the night at Calgary. The papers gave
the temperature as 36 below at that point, so you
can imagine we are having a beastly mean trip.
Well dear, we are about to leave now so I'll stop. I
hope you will have written me by the time I get to
home camp about the 18th, Yours Lou.

Dora was in tears by the time she scanned the letter. She read it again, imagining his bright eyes, glow-
ing with enthusiasm. Home? What home was he talking
about? Surely all the exhaustion, confusion and fatigue
made it impossible for him to think clearly. He noted his

travel as best he could, sharing his frustrations, but nothing was worth the changes she sensed in these recent letters. Still, she would not move! It would be foolhardy in the extreme to subject their family to the area Lou had described. Most importantly, she feared for his health.

His business carried on, with help from Frank who provided structure and monitored week to week finances. Lou's brother Joe was the physical backbone and kept contact with customers.

But surely, this was the most discouraging message, Canada! The country to the north sounded far away. She didn't want to hear the details, even though this was all for her and their family, the family which she alone nurtured in Ogden. Why couldn't he see that? Perhaps he did.

One crackly phone conversation revealed that distance, misunderstood words and letters crossing too late for a timely response, was the norm. She fairly shouted into the phone and then regretted the goodbye: "Is this going to be our way of life, Lou? Nothing seems to change except it gets worse. Jesse isn't well. Can't you come home for good? Surely Corey Bros. sees your value, but they're taking advantage of you. You are not a young man, Lou, camping and riding the rails, spending days on horseback, grueling even for a young man. And your precious back. I remember how I used to think I helped when you had done a cord of wood and I could at least apply liniment and warm cloths. But you are now hundreds of miles away, maybe a thousand, I don't know. Come home, Lou!"

There had been no response.

Several days later, Dora tried to set a lighter tone by phone, hoping the connection would be more reliable.

"Oh Lou, I received a note from Burton French via Frank the other day about the two of them going to the World's Fair in St. Louis."

There was only a slight pause before Lou responded, not bothering to soften his answer to her. "That's just the ticket for us, Pol, let's go to the World's Fair." The thump of Lou's fist on whatever hard surface was in front of him, rang over the phone line.

Dora hung up softly. Soon after, Lou called back, commenting wryly that the trip might be beyond their reach, but he understood how enticing it looked to her.

Dora couldn't help musing, where did Lou fit in? If not part of his own family and the business he had created, he had once had a niche in Ogden without question. From the Elks Brotherhood to the canyon fellowship, Lou had sloughed off these ties which, at one time, had energized him.

Burton French's canyon home on a small island in the middle of the Ogden River was a particular respite for fly enthusiasts and professional men who saw the outdoors as healthful and restorative. The men quoted from and passed around *Field and Stream* articles as they relaxed in Burton's comfortable but rustic cabin. The interior was decorated to a man's taste, with rough and nubby fabrics. Indian rugs of various sizes covered the floor. There was a large fireplace faced with river rock where the men burned wood harvested from property nearby. An assortment of tackle and hunting trophies hung on the wall, some from the beamed ceiling. Burton prepared the simple meals himself. The cabin was a sanctuary where confidences were held sacred.

Dora called Frank and invited him for tea the next day. He often came to the house on business, all entirely proper. His figure was a familiar one on 28th Street, whether or not Lou was in town.

Dora greeted Frank at the side door and ushered him into the room adjoining the small kitchen, where a table was set with her best tablecloth and napkins. After wishing him good morning, she hung his hat and stepped into the kitchen where she had a tray prepared with tea, sandwiches and some miniature sweet rolls baked that morning.

Frank's quick appraisal of her faded flowered dress increased the protective desire he struggled to hide from her, and from himself.

"Here, let me help you with that, Dora." Frank lifted the heavy tray before she grasped the handles and placed it on the table.

Dora could not help notice how gracefully Frank moved. His build was stocky compared to Lou, and not as tall, but still a fine figure of a man. She chided herself for this less than seemly observation.

"Let's eat first, Frank." She quickly sat down facing him. "I haven't had anything but coffee and I'm a little hungry." A nervous cough escaped her, and she mumbled, "Pardon, Frank."

Dora nodded toward the mantel and said, "Remind me to return your copy of *Sister Carrie*. I've had it for ages. Lou was taken with the illustration and thought I might enjoy it, which I did. It made me think about challenges others face, those not as fortunate as I am."

Frank was glad to see a smile. Dora didn't look well. "The few papers I have for you to look over can wait, Dora, and I have a check for you, reflecting rent from the rooms over the store. I just had the tenant make it out to you since Lou's out of town, just avoids my putting it in the bank, as I can cosign, don't mean to go on and on." Frank was noticeably flustered but Dora took no notice. "Of course, you can write a check any time you have a need."

Dora poured the tea, adding milk and sugar. She knew exactly how Frank liked his tea. She preferred coffee with sugar and cream. Lou was a black coffee drinker and always reached for an appropriated mug from Blocks at the back of the cupboard, rather than Dora's china.

Frank began with promising news. "Lou called last night and said he had contracted for a substantial sale."

Dora barely attended to what Frank was going on about, that Lou had contracted for a sale. She didn't care about these details. They were as dry as dust. "Frank, I try to understand, I really do."

Her soft words floated between them. Frank took her hand. She withdrew it but without any awkwardness. Frank wanted to again take her hand, stand and draw her to himself, crushing her to his chest.

"I would rather not have the sale and have him home more." She poured more tea and took a small bite of her sandwich.

Frank had devoured three of the small delicacies. He was hungry, having walked up the hill from his office, not taking time for lunch at Blocks; in fact, forgetting completely an appointment he had that day to meet Fred Keisel at the Broom lunchroom.

"Dora, let me say a few things about Lou." Dora closed her eyes tightly. "A lot of this you know already. Rugged? I've seen him in rugged conditions. I only went north with him twice, but I watched him mount a horse in an instant, and I know he often rides for hours in all kinds of weather, sheltered or not, or finds a logging camp farther up the line. I couldn't live like that."

Dora shook her head slowly.

"Until you observe him as I have, ready to heave himself up into a box car, making sure I was comfortable at a base camp; I talked to the men he works with, you have only an inkling of what he's trying to do for you all here. I knew at one point he would get off, grab a few hours of sleep in a bed others had probably slept in, down gallons of coffee and have cigarettes for his breakfast and no change of clothes."

Dora knew all this and fairly cringed to hear the full litany which Frank spewed out at her.

"Once I watched him write out a deal for trees on the side of a box car, the two words 'cutting' and 'dragging' underlined in heavy grease pencil. It made my head swim, yet he was so sure of himself."

For an instant, Frank wondered if he were pleading Lou's case in too convincing a manner, but he went on, "I know of many instances when he never asked anyone to do more than he did. Of course, he comes home to you," Frank gestured broadly with his hand indicating the food on the table, "to refreshment and being with his children and a feeling of well done."

Dora covered her face with her hands.

"Lou sees the future and knows that before the dams and canals come, the hard work he does, the railroads have to be there and . . ."

"I understand, Frank. I know how you feel and I know his reasons, but they are hard for me to accept. I need him to be here. What sense does it make to be so far from home, to make a better home, here?"

And in that instant Frank read her thoughts. He penetrated the insulation which she had surrounded herself with, from care of her children and home to ward duties and ties to her family in Mound Fort. As she returned his gaze, Frank was convinced that Lou was not in her thoughts.

The telephone rang and she turned from Frank to answer it. This broke the current which had been exchanged between them. She responded with patience to whatever issue needed her attention on the phone.

Frank knew he was not the center of her life. He shouldn't think it, but he did, and he wanted desperately to be just that. While Dora continued with her telephone conversation, Frank left quietly, hat in hand. He stood for a moment on the familiar side porch. He shuffled a bit as though waiting for Dora to call him back in, like a child outside the principal's office; listening a moment to the familiar voice, but finally he left. He would have other opportunities to show understanding. What he wanted to say, but of course did not, was that he could offer Dora and the children a future, which could not be matched by Lou's dreams. In fact, his dreams would be in jeopardy if Lou didn't take better care of himself.

Later that evening in his comfortable study, Frank ignored his normal dinner hour. Work from the office that he had brought home lay neatly arranged on his desk. Several matters requiring his attention caught his eye. This being Thursday, it was his practice to clear up what he could at home, leaving Friday to prepare for court on Monday, and a vestry meeting on Tuesday.

In his well-ordered approach to his profession of some fifteen years, restorative activities would have his attention on the weekend. He had contemplated time with friends at Burton French's place in the canyon and dinner at the Weber Club Saturday evening with newly appointed judge, Randolph Kenney.

Restless, he arose from his chair and walked to stand before the fireplace. He stared into the sputtering flames. Frank was at turns exhausted and energized. Although she would never accept it, in his mind Dora was his, God help him.

For Frank, absent was any thought of what his friends enjoyed as married men. He had never given it fair hearing or, for that matter, how Lou, his friend, might have felt as a youth, courting Dora. This was anathema to him. Unknown and unsought, even in his imagination, was their long history together. For his part, going forward was what mattered.

Frank abruptly returned to his desk, determined to finish his work. Afterward he would prepare a light meal for himself before retiring, and possibly, enjoy a glass of port.

⌒

Several days after meeting with Frank, Dora wrote to Lou: *My dear husband, Jesse isn't any stronger, he moans every move he makes. Bess Wheelwright said her mother says not to worry, he is just having growing pains, something about the long leg bones, have you ever heard of that? Did you have them? Anyway I've called for the Dr, Dr. Kemp, just moved down from Logan. Anyway, your mother is still in Chicago visiting friends.*

Last week the Tribes came by to see Viv and his wife, who are here from Denver. I served homemade pie, cake, beer, which Viv enjoys, and coffee. It was a nice evening though now the parlor smells of cigars. Viv hasn't been a follower of the Word of Wisdom at least as far as smoking, and he does enjoy an occasional beer, so I had it for him.

Still I will miss my brother when they are permanently in Denver. I was dressed in my green costume. Do you remember it? I can only believe that you would not, having seen it for at least four years. I'm sorry, my dear, I didn't mean to call your attention to other times and activities. I just at times feel sad that I have no activities to enjoy with my handsome husband wearing the green costume or something more, mode 'o day, remember that term?

Oh, did you read in the paper about Mrs. Malan, you know they are related through my mother's family. Jesse received your telegram for his birthday and it meant more to him than a book on the planets, which Frank bought for him. It made him very happy. Lou, we are lonely for you. I've paid the bills for the driver and from the pharmacy and a small charge from the confectioners at The Broom. Yours and ever, D. P. S. Frank stopped by for tea, he admires your drive. I wish you could drive on home, ha, no surprise to you, I am sure. D

The New Columbia Hotel, Shoshone, Idaho, 1/10/05

My Dear Dora, I received your letter today written yesterday. Wrote you a line last night that I expect you will receive today. I was in camp all week. A. B. Corey was only a day there and then came up here returning yesterday. I know this will be the way it will be. He can't stay on the work like W.W. and he wants me with him. He asked how long I would need to be here and for me to hurry back to camp. Corey is doing very nicely here, seems to gauge the work and grip what has to be done, and I shall not have much bookkeeping to keep me away from the work, so I expect to go down there about day after tomorrow. I assured A. B. that I would be there by that time.

Dora had a difficult time even following what Lou was saying. Did down "there" mean Ogden? She feared that "there" was the campsite. What drivel!

We have a hard piece of work. We are running into rocky land and I have had to telegraph for much heavier plows than we thought would be necessary, and also for steel and powder as we shall have considerable rock work. I think we will do fairly well on this piece of work, but we have had to spend lots of money in new outfit- horses, tents and tools to start with. We have here a much larger outfit than we have in Canada and it is expected we shall secure a lot more work.

Dora knew that these bits of information did not refer to logging, but construction. Dams, canals, rail bed preparation? She didn't know.

Glad you had such a nice time Sunday with all your visitors. My Sunday was spent largely on horseback riding alone over our ten miles of work and loosing myself time and time again in the ever-present sagebrush. I was follow- ing the canal line by the cross-section stakes and I would lose them and run all over the country before I could again get my bearings but I got through all right from one camp to another.

I don't want to do a thing under heaven to cause you a moment's pain or worry and I think you must believe this. I hope you are satisfied with me. I have tried to do for you all I am capable of doing, and want you to be as happy as

*any woman in this broad land. You are certainly to me the
one woman in the world, the mother of my babes, and you
must know I think this. There is nothing that would give
you pleasure that I would not secure for you, were I able.*

How on earth did Lou have the energy to write with
such intensity? She had been sent to the woodshed and
rightly so, complaining and, in his view, she may have
seemed absolutely wild to go to a party with him. Dora
was in tears, having gone the full range of anger, frustration and nearly moved to throw something across the
room. But in spite of herself, she gritted her teeth at the
boring reference to rock work, powder, tents and tools.
What did she care about these things? She cared about him.

As Lou's letter went on, he described the rail line
accessing both camps near the Snake River between
Shoshone and Twin Falls City, and sketched in his inim-
itable way the placement of rails and campsites, even
including some stick figures and scattered pine trees,
which made Sally, nearly twelve, laugh. Even this caused
Dora to tear up. He assured her that by phone and messenger, he would not be far from her if she needed to
talk to him. He implored her to write more often and she
faulted herself in this respect, always interrupted by one
thing or another. His closing words also sent her into a
state of yearning and regret and she accepted the scolding, for the moment at least:

*Well dearest, I guess I'll go to work on my books again
for a little while. I think I'll telephone you again tonight,
yours, Lou.*

March 3, 1905, My dear Lou, I was so glad to get your letter this mail. I was afraid you would not write after telephoning. Lou, you don't sound well, I'm reading between the lines I know, but, just tell me. I've packed my trunk and am ready to start the next train after you send for me. I do not even care to do my little housework. Jesse was quite bad last night again, vomiting, his temperature was only ninety-nine this morning though he has not attempted to get around at all today, eats fine. It is a relief to have Sally, she is so well and lovely. She had been staying next door. I wander from one house to the other, no ambition for anything. I do not suppose that Jesse will be able to attend school this year, though we can tutor him adequately.

It is much colder today. Was there any snow at Twin Falls? I just got the sound of your voice on the phone when you first rang up but the telephone girl said, "Hello, Shoshone" at least twenty times then she said, "He's at the barber shop." I remember when you wouldn't go anywhere but the barber shop at the Broom Hotel, what was the barber's name, Julio, wasn't it? Then you called again. I was on the phone all the time, then the phone girl said, "I can't get him yet from the barber shop. I'll ring you again." So, the operator here said, "I'll call when he rings." Well it was a full half hour before the message came. I was about to despair of talking with you and I was consoling myself with the idea that I had at least heard your voice at first, when you were trying to get me, when the final call came. I'm saving the Standard Examiners. Do you want me to box them to send to you? I guess you will be in Shoshone until Friday morning then to Twin Falls for an indefinite time. Is A.B. there yet?

Sally has come from Weston's with some licorice and she and Jesse are sucking it for dear life. She told me to write it to you. I made them some popcorn balls. I want to do something for you. Now don't tell me just be contented. Here I sit, hour after hour by a warm fire, thank you for providing it, and just cannot be happy. Jesse is trying to wash Sally's face but he cannot get the best of her. I had to get him a pair of skates, size 9½, cost sixty cents and worth the price. All the boys have them. Just now Jesse is lying on the floor trying to hypnotize Pete with a piece of candy. Well, he was watching Pete looking at the candy and drawing nearer and nearer and Pete let the saliva drop right in Jesse's eye. Oh, he was so mad, he is half crying now. It wasn't Pete's fault so I didn't punish him. Our dog certainly likes to be in the middle of things and he is so gentle with everybody.

I can't think of anything to say except, well, when I'm writing I just say what we're doing here and it would be so much better if you were here. I do love you so dearly but I will try to be sensible so that you will love me again. You must not fail to write me either. Perhaps I could meet you in Shoshone for a day or two? Truly, your Dora.

Chapter Twenty-Four
A Lunch in Town

At ten past one, Frank waited with the patience of a lover for Dora, trying to remember that she was his friend's wife. She had suggested Blocks on the east side of Washington Avenue.

Blocks was the place in Ogden, much nicer than the L. and W., where journalists, lawyers and merchants congregated, took their breakfast, often had lunch and met with colleagues. Opened in 1901, their specialty was wholesome food served with promptness. The ceiling was very high and twelve lights hung over the area; the walls were creamy lemon, shiny and serviceable.

Oak flooring covered most of the room except for behind the U-shaped counter, where beige and brown tile had been installed. Wooden booths formed the perimeter and scattered tables filled the remaining space. Sturdy coat racks had been secured near the door, allowing for heavy wool outer wear in cold weather, and hats and umbrellas appropriate for the season. Dowels were screwed into the heavy molding over which were draped the local papers, usually one each from Denver, Chicago, San Francisco and St. Louis. An adjacent sign warned patrons not to remove papers from the premises and to watch their ashes.

Men found it convenient to have breakfast at Blocks. Mrs. Block's waffles with tinned fruit, fresh fruit in season, were as popular as her funnel cakes. Thin and light, they were served not in a stack but attractively arranged in a spiral on a large plate, buttered generously with sprinkled sugar or Mrs. Block's fruit syrup. Noon was also a busy time and lawyers between cases, merchants and shoppers found the booths inviting for conversation. The counter seating provided a quick nourishing bowl of chile or soup with a roll and a break from the hectic commercial scene.

At the front were smaller tables for two overlooking Washington Avenue. Potted palms softened the angular space, and the silo size coffee urns and the aroma of rolls, bacon and sizzling meat provided warmth. The restaurant windows allowed views of businesses across the street and a frequently passing trolley. A rather imposing bank stood on the west side of the street, while flanking Blocks stood a bookstore established by the Croft family. Several specialty shops, among them Annie's millinery, provided additional choice in friendly competition with Z.Cs.

Frank glanced up frequently listening for the swish of the door which would signal Dora's arrival. He had walked over twenty minutes earlier from his office in the new city hall. Finally, his patience rewarded, he put down his paper as Dora came toward him. As she held out her gloved hand, he admired the soft brown suit she wore. It was modest in cut, ecru lace setting off the simple collar. A slight rim of dark plaid accented the cut of the bodice, the same plaid fabric bordering the rim of her hat. He had no doubt that his sister Annie was responsible for this creation.

"Frank, you are so good to take time away from your office to meet me." As she seated herself, Frank signaled for Mabel to bring his order, for an instant distracted by the faint scent of lavender. This was late lunch time when pie and coffee were common. Frank was somewhat surprised when Dora ordered tea.

Frank was seen by others in Blocks as an established friend of the Jensen couple. A bit older than Lou and a lodge brother, his presence beside Dora, in Lou's absence, was unremarkable, even as he briefly covered her hand with his own.

Pulling her hand away, she removed her gloves. She placed a book wrapped in green paper tied with twine on the table. "An impromptu gift for Lou, a copy of *The Virginian* by Owen Wister. I know he will enjoy it. Have you read it, Frank?"

Frank, captivated as he was by simply sitting at the table with Dora, just shook his head. A trolley jangled by as Frank watched Fred M. Nye walk north toward his store where Frank bought most of his clothes. Fred waved to him in a friendly manner and made a mental note to set up a fishing outing at Burton French's canyon lodge, a common meeting place. Many considered fishing their main recreational activity along with duck hunting and motoring, a somewhat new avocation gaining in popularity. Burton French himself walked by as he exited the eating area and tipped his hat to Dora.

Frank's back was to the interior of the eating area and he didn't see this attention to Dora. He faced the window to spare Dora the western glare, having heard Lou talk about how sensitive her eyes were and how she disliked wearing her glasses.

Frank's coffee sat almost untouched, as did their pie. He noticed Mrs. Block eyeing their table. He hoped she would not come closer to find out why they weren't eating more enthusiastically. Tight lipped, her hair coiled in a braided bun, nothing escaped Mrs. Block's attention as a savvy restauranteur. She was well acquainted with Frank who always left a generous tip.

Dora wore amber ear bobs. Frank had picked them out himself while shopping with Lou at a jewelry store on 25th Street near Washington. The jeweler John Smalley had been in business since shortly after he arrived from England in 1898, and Lou was one of his first customers. Mr. Smalley was also a watchmaker, and Lou had sent many friends to him. In fact, Dora had purchased a handsome watch there the previous year as a Christmas gift for Lou.

At first Lou had leaned more toward a pair of dark filigree earrings set with amethyst. But Frank convinced him that the amber in another pair would pick up the glint in Dora's eyes. Mr. Smalley agreed, and the sale was made. Lou was as pleased as Dora with the selection.

Frank, observing an Indian walking down the street, gestured for Dora to turn in her chair quickly to see the man. He wore a turquoise velvet shirt, tan trousers and work boots. His hair was cut chin length.

Frank said, "Poor fellow. I see him often near city hall. He's something of a fixture."

"Actually, Frank, I think Lou knows him, or his mother does." Dora took a sip of her cooled tea, placing the cup with a delicate clink in the saucer. She then motioned for the girl to bring more hot water.

Frank admired this initiative on her part. He wouldn't have expected it.

Dora said, "That man makes determinations based on his own lights."

"Now where did that come from?" Frank clinked his cup in its saucer and waited for more.

"You forget that I am a duly registered teacher in the city, have been for many years and am well acquainted with the works of Cooper."

"Well, *The Leatherstocking Tales* is a favorite of mine," Frank said.

She smiled over the edge of her tea cup and Frank imagined she was actually flirting with him.

Frank continued, "Well, my interest in Cooper has to do with his naval perspectives," Frank said. "His works, and Roosevelt's, keep me at my desk longer than they should, given my case requirements, but seriously I think naval power, the kind Great Britain has, will be even more important in future wars."

Dora laughed lightly. "Frank, how did we get on such a serious conversational path?"

In Frank's mind, any train of conversation would be delightful with Dora. "Well, then, continue discussing your references to an Indian's lights."

Dora looked up, turning her head as if she were looking for the server, "Oh yes, well, I can't speak with any depth on that, but I do believe they have moral insight."

As a girl in a stiff grey apron came toward them, Frank stood to pay their bill. Then he resumed his seat, not anxious to bring their time to an end. But he seemed to have lost the clever line he thought he had initiated, changing the subject completely, placing his elbow on the table and leaning his chin on his fist. "Tell me, why don't you call Eliza, your mother-in-law, Mother Jensen, Mrs. J, something like that," he asked Dora. "You know she's all bark."

Frank saw Dora wince slightly. He would have done anything to have recalled the hasty comment, realizing that, though he thought he knew Eliza well because of their business dealings, the abrupt change of subject didn't have the effect he sought.

He pushed, "Perhaps Eliza?"

Dora laughed. "Eliza? Never. I just avoid the need, and no, not Mother Jensen either, in fact, I sometimes just use Mrs. Jensen."

More serious concerns and issues seemed to slip away. Frank was powerless to guide the conversation elsewhere, now that the one-sided illusory courting dance was spreading like a web around them. Always in control of his thoughts and phrases, Frank sensed that his grasp had slipped. He was as overcome as a schoolboy in Dora's presence.

"Even Eliza?" Frank was squinting in the sun and turned his chair sideways. He was sure that Dora didn't notice his discomfort, and he wouldn't have admitted this to her for the world. The changed position of his chair allowed Frank to observe, in the mirrored column panel near them, an image of a laughing Dora, the delightful expression on her face for a time, a smile directed toward him alone.

She laughed again, there was that incomparable musical trill, throaty, rather than shrill in the manner of so many women he knew. "I just told you, Frank, never Eliza, never."

Dora shook her head and the ear bobs jiggled flirtatiously. She undoubtedly would have blushed at the thought that she was playing the coquette. Of course, if she were truly his Dora, their conversations would often have just this type of playfulness. Was she unaware of how adorable she looked to him? He longed to ring up Fords' Photographic Studio and schedule a sitting for her that very day; an absurd idea, of course.

Later, as Frank escorted Dora through the door to the sidewalk area, the couple saw Frank's sister Annie walking briskly, crossing the street and heading for her shop. Although the weather was unseasonably warm, she carried a light knit jacket over her arm. She wore a long tweed skirt and cream shirtwaist with softened sleeves, rather than the stiff balloon type some women felt constrained, by fashion, to wear.

A St. Louis artist friend of Annie's, back from a recent trip to Paris with her family, had shown Annie sketches of working women there, unimpeded by longer skirts, wearing serviceable pumps rather than lace up shoes. They were therefore freed from mincing steps but could stride along as Annie walked, with an athletic rhythm.

With almost physical pain, Frank let Dora slip from his light grasp on her elbow as she hurried to catch her trolley. She turned to him with a smile that only wounded him further, but he waved a hearty goodbye.

ᐅ

Dora had become increasingly convinced that the last thing she wanted to do was follow Lou to Canada or even Montana, just inside the US border. These destinations seemed to her uncivilized outposts, years from providing the refinements and opportunities which her children deserved. For the afternoon at least, Dora had been her own woman, escorted by Frank who chose her company over any of the other women in Ogden, those younger and of marriageable age.

Dora was glad she had not shared with Frank her suspicions about a pregnancy, why the aromatic coffee and rolls in Blocks had affected her the way they had. Frank was a good friend but not an intimate one and, after all, a man. But to be fair, an attractive man, whose every attention was directed toward her every utterance. What would her mother-in-law think? She stepped down from her trolley and hurried on toward home.

A few days after Dora's meeting with Frank, Lou came back home after a quick trip to Shoshone.

Dora wanted to re-integrate him into downtown Ogden, where he seemed to have lost interest. She called him at his office, imagining he might feel good to be there again. She pictured him sitting at his desk, his long legs propped up on a short stack of papers, holding the phone in his own peculiar way, able to write with either hand if needed, jotting down notes even as he paged through the latest copy of *Field and Stream*.

"Lou, meet me at Mrs. Keller's hair-dressing parlor." Dora heard him humming. She continued, "It's on Washington near 24th. We'll have lunch." A slight tone of desperation crept into her voice despite striving for nonchalance.

"Now where is it and what kind of parlor is it? Oh, I guess this is to get you gussied up for Release Society," Lou said, his tone lulling.

Dora recognized the unmistakable exhalation of smoke into the mouthpiece. She thought of the stain on his fingers due to smoking, heavier at one time than now, but more as he traveled, she suspected.

"Lou, you're just pretending you don't know it's Relief Society not Release. F not S, and I've been elected secretary. You know I get my hair done there."

His barely audible chuckle was reassuring. "You don't mean you get your hair done at Relief Society?"

"Of course not, now you're just being silly. You know I get my hair done at Mrs. Keller's. . . . Lou, are you listening? We'll have lunch at Blocks. Surely you haven't lost your taste for pastry, even with all your travels."

She thought about her homemade apple pies, which long ago he had devoured, sweet as they were, with more sugar on top; then catching her in his arms, brushing her cheeks with his scratchy face, both of them enjoying the sticky closeness. Did he ever recall now such madness in the kitchen after the children were asleep? Even after Darling and Rennie were gone, hadn't life been good?

"I'll wait just inside the door. I don't want my hair mussed in the wind." She hung up, knowing he had heard every word and would meet her. But she was slightly perturbed and didn't know why. Could it have been because she remembered how Lou had loosened her hair to see the wind play in it, as she pretended irritation that he knew was artifice to only entice him further?

All was at peace on 28th Street. Eliza left for Chicago to commune with like-minded women whose focus was women's rights. She was not shy about her opinions, but became more outspoken the farther east she traveled. Dora looked forward to family time with Lou, seeing how the children benefitted, and in the reflected light of that, she was resigned to be secondary, but Lou returned north to Idaho, first to Blackfoot then to Shoshone.

Chapter Twenty-Six
Letters

Alberta Hotel, 3/24/1906

Arrived safely. Leave for Wetaskiwin in the morning. Both Mrs. Coreys are going up and, as soon as I get there, I will see how things are and have you come up. I see we have all of a year's work so you may start at once getting ready. I love you all. Goodbye, Lou.

This was one of the most puzzling letters Lou had written. Cold, formal, giving an order, and Dora didn't like it. The goodbye, too, was cold. She couldn't shake the feeling of unease and could only hope the next letter would be different. But regarding Lou's outrageous scheme to move north? She wasn't going to do it.

Then, out of the blue, he offered to meet in Shoshone. The couple had three days there, the first time without their children that Dora could remember. The New Columbia was not The Broom but any place was somehow magical, so harried had their life become. She imagined long talks into the night, intimacy rekindled, dreams for the future, talk of a new son or daughter, but the magic she sought to weave was overshadowed by Lou's talk about his plans for them. Any illusions Dora had about changing his mind were dashed by his insistence that she see the land.

She didn't look forward to the journey back to Ogden alone.

Calgary, on Corey Brothers letterhead, 5/27/06, Lou wrote:

Dear Pol, I wish you to have the Standard Examiner *come to Camrose, Alberta and write me there as well, quick. I want to know how you all are. Now I shall be ready for you just as soon as you can make it. You may do with the house as you wish, rent or lock up. I wish you could get up courage to ask George Malan for an employee rate to Butte for you and the children. I don't think he would mind, and it would be a great help to us. Then you have your rates to Letheridge and I think I will have no bother to get a pass from there up here. And Camrose is only twenty-five-miles farther or is it further? I can never remember but you can set me right as you always do. Now hurry, I'll know about the pass tomorrow. Yours truly, Lou.*

Dora sat down, needing to reread every sentence. She was to start at once to get ready. The paper was now to come there, Camrose is in Alberta, Canada. They didn't live in Canada. They lived in Ogden, Utah, they had a home, neighbors, Lou had a business with Joe. "Do with the house as you wish." How could he write "the house"? This was their home. Now she was to rent it out or lock it up; for how long?

Her tears came in jerky sobs. Aloud she tried to reel off the reality of her situation and in her mind contrast that with Lou's perception. Did he remember she was pregnant? Did he think Jesse should be taken out of school? A long trip with ten-year-old Sally would be difficult, needing as she did structure and routine. And what about sleeping and eating; easy for a man to grab coffee and miss meals but she had needs to remain healthy through her pregnancy, and Sally would not do well in a different town each day. Of course, Jesse would have to stay with Eliza, or even Delia could take that responsibility. She felt she was getting pulled into his crazy thinking. She must either get some sleep or talk to someone. She stopped herself. She would wait to hear further, but she felt bone chilled with fear.

Just two weeks later, Lou wrote from Calgary again. *Dear love, I'm enclosing a pass from Letheridge to Wetaskiwin so you may get ready as soon as you wish and come up. I would bring some bed linen and table linen and knives etc.; we will have to buy a small store and a tent but I guess there is no other way. The two Mrs. Coreys will have to do the same and I guess we can put up with what they have to endure.*

At this point, Dora would have inquired about the degree of pregnancy either of the women, the younger being in her late forties, sustained. For herself, she judged she would deliver in August. What did he mean by a small store? An outfit of staples, the same as a Great Plains crossing, should she bring a gun? And the mention of a tent disturbed her the most. She had no words for him on that subject.

In August Lou had written, *I'm very busy writing contracts, buying goods and we will leave in the morning for camp. You will have to write me a few days before you leave so I can meet you over at Wetaskiwin. I won't be able to come to Letheridge for you this time I hardly think, but I will arrange for someone to meet you. If Mrs. Tribe can come up with some scratch for a ticket or buy your own. And it won't cost so much more which you could save by carrying your meals in a basket and using your Pullman only at night. It will be a tiresome trip for you but you will have a half day and a night at Calgary for rest as your train gets here at noon and leaves at 7:45 next morning.*

Dora knew Mrs. Tribe socially but had no understanding of arrangements to be made with her for the trip. Dora couldn't imagine that she would pay for Dora's ticket. She would just pay for it herself.

Lou continued in his letter, *As I said, do as you like about the house and take the time you need before coming as it is quite cold here yet, and will be stormy for some time but I shall be very happy to see you soon, your Lou.*

૨

Dora stared at, and in fact held onto, the pass from Canadian Pacific Railway Company, after she received it by mail. She also noted that it would be void after September 25th. Dora counted the days, but once Lou's meticulous directions arrived, she made up her mind to make the trip. A terse conversation with Eliza put her mind at ease.

"I see no reason, Dora, for Jesse to miss any school and I will continue to tutor him as we move into the summer." Looking at Dora, half expecting a comment at least, she pressed on, "And if I travel east to Chicago, why, I'll just take him with me."

Eliza didn't understand much of her son's thinking. Although he had been competent looking over her land purchase in Montana, she had no understanding why he would talk of moving his family there. This trip of Dora's with little Sally was to her mind a useless trek. Nevertheless, she would do all she could to help Dora prepare and she saw to it that Dora had ample money tucked in her jersey, sewn into an Eliza designed pocket.

The directions from Lou were numbered:

1. Pack trunk

2. Go to depot, buy ticket, secure berth

3. Get someone, probably Joe, to carry the trunk, in the wagon to depot for train going north day of departure. You and Sally ride in a carriage

4. Arrive at depot, check trunk and be sure to get sleeper. Give porter ticket to find berth

5. Rise next morning at seven, go into diner, order a small steak, coffee with mush with cream for Sally.

6. Ride until 3:30 pm

7. Give baggage master check for trunk and fifty cents to be transferred to Great Northern depot

8. Arrive Butte 4 pm, take street car uptown to rest, eat, take car back to depot

9. Buy ticket for 10.00 from Butte to Letheridge. Sign full names Dora Barlow Jensen, Jane Ellen Jensen

10. Take ticket and check trunk to Letheridge

11. Get on train about eight pm, ride until three am, arrive Great Falls

12. Take bus to Grand Hotel, secure bed and ask night clerk to call at six am

13. Rise and slip out for breakfast, then get on the bus at the hotel

14. Take train and ride to Letheridge

15. Arrive Letheridge about 11 pm, wait in depot for two hours and buy ticket

16. Check trunk to Calgary, arrive McLeod at about 9 pm, stay there until 2 am (I know it's hard but you can do it)

17. Get on the car, stay there until 11 am and you will be in Calgary and I will meet you.

Dora was numb as she reread the particulars of her ordeal. The phrase "Stay there until 2 am." was reread until it sunk in.

~~

Dora did travel to Montana with ten-year-old Sally. The journey was rigorous but not beyond Dora's considerable stamina. She recalled stories Eliza had told of crossing the plains in 1868, when she was pregnant with Lou. The studio photograph of twenty-year-old Eliza holding a naked Lou on her lap, was a testament to her endurance. Dora's difficulties and inconveniences paled in comparison to those Eliza encountered.

For one thing, Dora would travel by train rather than walking. If departure times were difficult, at least she had the companionship of Sally, who proved a more compliant traveler than Dora would have thought. Snacking instead of regular meals was a departure from routine, but neither was the worse for it. Thanks to the ability of the railroad to carry food grown on the coast to the interior, Dora could purchase fresh fruit to augment their simple bread and jam meals. Cold apple pie for breakfast, with coffee for Dora and milk for Sally, was adequate. Ten-year-old Sally enjoyed the many soft cloth books which Dora had tucked into her satchel. The pictures captured the child's interest; Dora added to the mix by crafting her own tales of a giant mouse named Herbert and a tiny brown bear dressed in knee pants and a green weskit.

Several weeks later, her pregnancy discomfort lessened on her way back to Ogden. If anything, relief may have played a part in her feeling that, though she might travel to Montana again, there would be no permanent change of address.

Conditions had been rustic. Rather than a tent, the family had use of a small house. It was tolerable in late spring but, in Dora's opinion, not suitable as fall approached and winter loomed ahead with many weeks of isolation a possibility. The linens and other provisions she had brought made their sleeping arrangement more like home. Facilities for washing were more primitive, but Lou did all he could to provide some privacy for Dora. The couple talked intimately into the night as Sally slept on a cot on the other side of the table. They had tried out names for the baby, John Kay or David Kay, for a boy and Dora's choice, Dinah Eliza, if the baby were another girl.

⌒

John Kay Jensen was born August 16th in Ogden in the house on 28th Street. From that day forward, their son was always called Jack. Eliza the proud deliverer, Lou on his way south at least, and Dora, used to his absence, didn't register any dismay. She was surrounded by caring family who welcomed Lou when he also arrived. He held this newest son with tears in his eyes, tagging him his own "banner boy."

Dora felt sure Lou would stay through fall, perhaps for months after, but she was to be disappointed once again.

Chapter Twenty-Seven
Nan

She was called Nan. Lou first met her at the door of McCleary's boarding house in Butte. She wore a faded brown and yellow print dress. He saw only one other outfit, a pale muslin bodice with a dark green skirt, in the year and some months he lived there. She wore her hair braided, arranged high on her head in the French manner, but because of its coarseness, unruly strands framed her face like a wispy veil. Atop her braid was a stiff white caplet she wore when on duty, as did her cousin Bessie at the front counter, the only show of their station. Her cousin said it was like a nurse's cap only for food service, but she wore it with pride.

As she served Lou at a table one morning, he noticed her hands marked by kitchen duties and cleaning. Only later was he aware of all the extra service those hands provided, cleaning his room for example, mending the boarders' clothing, sewing miles of opened seams and patches on fabric rough and thick. All this wore on her hands in part to earn money for her son Tommy's board. Tommy was always dressed in clean jackets and trousers cut down from those given to her by former boarders as they moved away.

At first Lou only kidded with her, but soon his eyes lingered. He had told her in a friendly way about his family, spoken mostly over the top of his newspaper. He didn't mention that the last letters he had written Dora, full of his enthusiasm, had gone unanswered. He assumed Dora was too engaged with their new son to write him letters. In that Lou was correct, and he had read in one of her letters that Jack recently had endured a sudden bout of whooping cough but had made a sound recovery.

Nan was reticent at first, but over the next few weeks she smiled more at Lou and was not as curt in her service routine. Promptness rather than friendliness was the standard, travelers not usually being given to informal conversation with servers, but most likely having duties or destinations which called them.

One night Lou came up to his room to find Nan there, hanging up his shirts, which she had laundered herself. They were not folded and wrapped in paper as they usually were.

Lou's voice was of a different timbre than Nan was used to hearing in the lunchroom. "I told you or Tommy to take my shirts down the street to Chin's to be laundered." Lou's lack of control far outpaced the infraction, if it was that, but Nan's answer equaled his.

Hands on hips, she answered, "I don't see why it matters that I did them myself, but I'll not do it again, Lou." Once this had been said, this breach of propriety, she was near tears as she sped from the room.

Stunned, Lou heard the brief exchange in his head like an echo. Did he say what he said? Did she reply in the manner he witnessed, hands on hips, looking at him directly and calling him Lou, rather than Mr. Jensen?

The next morning Nan's voice was low but forceful as she served him in the lunchroom. "I'll thank you not to seek lodging here next time you blow into town, Lou. I can't abide it."

Fearing a rise in volume, Lou glanced around the room. Only one couple was seated, but they left as they responded to what they might have sensed to be an accelerating exchange, even as Nan's next comment reached their ears.

"I came on the boat . . . ship, from Ireland knowing I was a girl in trouble, I came here nearly twelve years ago with Bessie." She nodded toward her cousin minding the till at the front entrance, receiving money from a patron.

"Bessie's uncle had offered me an opportunity of coming to Montana to run the boarding house with Bessie. He had just started, not nice like it is now, but we thought we could make a go of it. I had no family. Think what you will, Lou, but her folks took me in, like one of them, and didn't look down on me because of . . . you know. We were both ready for the adventure of it, too. I wanted no man, and besides I had Tommy by then."

Lou was embarrassed by Nan's frank recitation of her history. He imagined Dora's facial expression had she heard it.

"I hadn't been here a week." She shook her finger at Lou. "One week and Edward Krug, you won't know him, the better for you, started coming in." Another couple who had seated themselves nearby stopped talking as they sensed revelations to come. A pointed glare from Nan set them on a course of lively chatter. Lou jumped at the punctuation of the loud napkin snap which Nan used to clear the table surface of crumbs. There was no smile on Nan's face.

Her voice softened but her intensity remained. "Who can say why we look good to one another, but he looked good to me. When I found out he was to marry and— mind, he never gave me more than a wink and "bring the coffee, girl"—but still I saw him, never with his new wife, but he came here to eat and be waited on by me and always for breakfast. His wife too lazy to come with him in the morning, was the story I got from Bessie." She nodded toward the front counter.

"I could see no one else 'tis the pity, though Joel, your partner for a time, once asked me." She hitched up the bib of her apron and smoothed her collar. "Well, never mind, I didn't see myself helping to raise his two young-sters. I brought my own with me, so to speak, with no father and no marriage either."

During this outburst, she had plopped herself down across from Lou, having caught Bessie's eye at the front. She'd bring no one back toward them, showing patrons counter seats instead. The couple at the nearby table noiselessly moved toward the front to settle their bill.

Nan leaned toward Lou, her face inches from his. "Can't you talk, Lou? Do you have an idea about anything I've said?"

Recently Dora's letters, apart from news about the baby, had been peevish. She may have been still smarting from her trip north. She would not have to make the move. That was settled, but her letters were full of complaints, and all would be well if only Lou were home. Lou felt detached from Ogden. Letters from Frank which used to fire him up instead further distanced him from an Ogden dynamic he had at first sought. Add all that to the reality that Dora would never move. Dora was never going to move.

The place was nearly empty. Light snow was falling and men scurried back and forth, their boot steps muffled against the wooden walkways.

Without prelude, Lou took Nan's hand across the table, hoping her outburst was over. Nan's skin was shiny with heat, the hair around her face damp. Lou had never allowed Dora to do hard work. If he wasn't there, Eliza's housekeeper or Mabel Stokes helped her. This woman, Nan, carried heavy trays, cleaned, washed, scrubbed floors and clothes; yet he thought her fine, in truth thought her lovely. Now he captured both hands with no resistance and explored with his thumbs the contours of her reddened fingers.

So far from home, Nan had been very good to look at each day as she gave him a smile. He liked to see her move around the room, and sometimes he caught a trace of a carnation aroma about her. He had written to Dora about Mrs. Delaney, how kind she had been to him, she and her son Tommy who often ran messages for him and took his horse to the livery.

Lou bowed his head.

"Now are you going to have a prayer, Lou? Is that what I am, a poor woman to pray over?"

As he looked up, Lou saw tears crowded at the corners of her eyes. Her smile was slightly mocking. At least the temperature of her outburst was reduced, Lou thought.

He shook his head and patted her hand, "Oh, Nan." Surely, he had agonized over his feelings for Nan, not acted upon but felt just the same, and played them out in some detail when alone in his room, the room she cleaned and tidied daily. His imagination had been explicit about being alone in that very room with Nan.

She was fine. He was not. He knew this, had known it when he was a young boy, had confessed the same to Dora, even committed his feverish desire to her on paper. Lou was lonely beyond bearing. The letters from home were cold, as cold as long ago. For his own purposes, he remembered that stretch of time he wooed and courted the proper Miss Barlow. He had intimated, in every way he could, the intensity of his desires. She replied with stiff notes, barely acknowledging that he had moved her at all, placating him with a reference to her own warm response. He had asked that she not send such cold letters, echoing his request from nearly twenty years before, how cold and formal her letters had been. Now again, the letters came, shutting him out, stilted formal reports of the children, and whining, that too, and complaints about the rental money not being enough, and didn't she see, he did it all for her? His thoughts tumbled in his consciousness and mind even as he looked at Nan.

Lou pushed it all away in a matter of seconds as Nan moved to stand. He grasped her arm at the elbow. "Could we walk, take a jacket . . . the snow?" He motioned toward the front where Bessie stood.

Nan had told Bessie about Lou, how hard he worked, how he avoided Pruitts down the street. She saw him come and go, always pleasant no matter how tired, never so much as a leering glance or a joke like the other men often shared with her, men who assumed she had heard them all and knew even better ones.

Nan shook her head; the pins holding her braids glittered in the light. She had been smitten by Lou's blue green eyes, ash blond hair and, as she had told Bessie, the mouth she hungered for. And about how she had ached to be held; not like Tommy's father who took advantage of her, then left her to board the ship, still watching for him at the dock.

Lou stood and looked down at her.

She said, "No, Lou, I might be a fool and you might be too, but 'tis better not."

She avoided looking up at him, thinking of the impropriety of standing so close, her head well below his chin, as if meeting his eyes would cause her to lose whatever reserve she now struggled to maintain.

When she did finally raise her head to look up at him, she said, "So, it's your arms around me and where will that happen? Somewhere between here and the livery and you a married man and what is it, three children?"

Stung by her tone, he stepped back seconds from embracing her in the now empty room.

"Yes, two boys and a girl, the other two . . ." The other two he hadn't spoken about but was desperate to do so.

"I heard you met her at Shoshone, and she stayed for two weeks. Not an easy trip with children. Why don't you get her to come up here for a spell?" Nan flung the question at him.

Lou looked as though he wanted to confide in her, instead saying, "Do you want that?"

"No, I don't want to lay my eyes on her. I want to lay my eyes on you and 'tis the shame of my evil soul."

Lou stopped further talk with his hand gently placed in front of her mouth. Nan broke from his grasp and hurried from the room, the heels of her well-worn shoes scuffing across the floor as her pace became a run.

Bessie stood at the counter, casting a backward glance at Lou, shaking her head.

Lou steadied himself against the table before turning to walk slowly toward the front. He reached into his vest pocket for the price of his meal but didn't check the time. His time had run out. Nan despised him. He turned to the antler rack, retrieved his hat and coat and went out into the night.

⌒

Lou wanted to go home. Dora needed him, that was clear. But he also needed his wife.

Later as he sat on the edge of his bed, he waited without much hope. The knock was very soft. It was easily nine o'clock. When he had left to go out in the night, feeling terrible and chastened by Nan, he didn't check the time and when he came in, he took off his vest and hung it on the bench. The knock came again.

It couldn't have been Nan, but it was. As Lou opened the door, he could only say, "You haven't come to see me, not after tonight, but . . ."

She brushed against him as she entered, smelling of the cold outdoors. So, she had been out too. There was a dusting of snow as she let her shawl drop to the floor.

She sat on the bed and removed the white caplet, placing it on the bedside table. Her eyes never left his.

Lou put one knee on the bed and pulled down his worn leather suspenders. Then he waited. He placed his hands on her shoulders, his heart racing as he imagined all he had dreamed of coming true.

"Lou, I have decided." She reached for the caplet and held it in her hands turning it carefully, not to twist it.

"My boy is up late working on his lessons. Bessie is next door. I told him I was going out for some fresh air. Bessie will get him up in the morning to go to the kitchen to his work."

Nan rose and Lou stepped back, off balance. He didn't bar her way. Neither of them smiled.

"I will go for a while, Lou. Look at your watch." There was a shadow of a smile as she looked at his vest and knew the gold watch was in the pocket. Nan had teased Lou about how often he checked the time.

He remained standing. He wanted to prevent her from leaving. "You won't come back, Nan. Is that it?" His arms hung at his sides.

She stood on tiptoe to kiss him on his cheek, the brief scratch of his whiskers the first time she had felt his face. "I'll come with my dress for tomorrow and fresh linen for your bed." She looked at the pillow she fluffed that morning, and Lou imagined lying beside her there. "I'll be up early ready to go down to make your coffee, and then you can come down at your usual time."

"But . . . Bessie." Lou winced. He knew he was weak and chided himself. She would have to risk being seen, tell Bessie, lie to Tommy, then scurry back to him to satisfy his carnal needs, his uncontrollable desire for her. He had controlled himself, never went to Mercury Street or even down to Pruitts. Was it only Nan that he loved? He loved Nan as he had never loved Dora. He couldn't bear to think it, but it was true.

"Yes, Bessie knows. She knows that I'm coming to you, and she will wake Tommy in the morning and see he gets to work in the kitchen as I told you. He will not know where I am."

After stooping to retrieve her shawl, Nan slipped out of the door quickly. Lou held it and watched her reach the stairs, a small towel over her arm. He saw no one in the corridor.

In less than an hour she came through the door without knocking and placed her things, including a fresh caplet, on the chair. She had bathed. Her hair was still coiled but more loosely. She unbuttoned the bodice of her dress quickly.

Lou hadn't looked at his watch. He had sat on the bed for ten minutes after she left, before washing and brushing his teeth. He returned to sit on the bed, thinking of life hundreds of miles south, another life than what he lived now. He twisted his wedding ring until the inscription burned, then removed it and placed it on the table. Dora would never move to be with him, and tonight he knew he would never go back to stay.

His heart pounded in his chest as he waited until he felt on the floor the tapping of Nan's footsteps, so well did he know her rhythm, walking quickly along the carpeted hallway. He was on his feet and at the door to hold her as she came in.

⌒

"I won't break, Lou."

Lou stared out of the grimy window, the train chugging south once again to Ogden and Dora. He heard Nan's throaty lilt as she had said those words, "I won't break, Lou."

No, Nan didn't break, and he had put aside all reserve and moved with purpose, tenderness and energy he had forgotten he possessed; and joy without regret. They had only one night. How many times did he take the Lord's name in vain and only once had Nan's lips covered his as he did so. How many times had he folded sweet Nan in his arms and felt her breath on his neck as he whispered into her dewy back, "I'll come back, Nan."

The trees, hills, rocks moved by with boring repetition. He checked the time often, the watch given to him by Dora not so many years before. Lou had once loved the progression from Montana south, homeward.

Now it just took him farther away from Nan.

Chapter Twenty-Eight
Lou

Lou's return to Ogden brought a somewhat guarded response from Dora, at least at first. Over the next few weeks however, valuable distance was traveled in more ways than one. Lou gave long overdue attention to all three children, catching them up in his arms many times, although his first attentions were to Jack as the youngest, his "banner boy."

Jesse was reduced to giggles over his father's pitiful stick figures as he attempted a cartoon cowboy narrative. Sally sat on Lou's lap with her favorite picture books. Jack was warmly nuzzled by Lou at bedtime, a welcome accompaniment to stories, original ones from Lou. They were illustrated with sketches and sounds, whether train whistles, neighing horses, or clip-clopping hooves.

Dora could tell Lou was trying to make up for all the days and nights away from his family, but to her it seemed impossible and his warmth didn't extend to her. He would encourage the children to mind her or help with the table clearing, while giving her a smile, as if she were a favorite cousin staying with the family. At least, that's how it felt to Dora as she leaned against the kitchen door frame one afternoon, watching Lou making cocoa for the children.

As if trying to catch up with months of inattentiveness, within a week of his arrival, Lou attended an Elks meeting, lunched with Frank, was brought up to date on accounts at the store, and given an up to the moment read on town gossip. He paid what amounted to professional calls on leaders and neighbors, the Harris brothers, Jed Hatch, all with whom he had dealt before, sharing the particulars with Dora who was giddy at the thought of him re-entering Ogden society. She saw no reason why the progress couldn't accelerate. He even spent an afternoon with David Kay, his mentor, without whom Lou would not have started his business, modeled as it was on David's more expansive wholesale, grocery, grain and lumber company.

Dora was encouraged. And to her surprise, Lou engaged in homeowner activity at a rate not seen for years. These weren't the activities of a man not fully committed to his home. In letters, he had told her that she should sell or close up the house. But now, she thought, Lou couldn't possibly be thinking of selling or even renting their house, their home on 28th Street.

Lou's mother, Eliza, had mentioned to Dora, more than once, that she felt Lou's heart had moved north. But with Lou back home, Eliza as well as Dora warmed to Lou's idea, vividly described, of a rail trip north for all the family, just a short vacation in Montana, definitely not a permanent relocation.

In truth, Dora knew no one who took vacations, certainly not out of state. Frank and Annie's travels were understandable; they had come from a different background altogether.

Dora supposed that Lou intended, with this vacation idea, to show them the country that captivated him. The children indeed had been won over by their father's descriptions. Dora herself imagined gazing out of the train window as Lou provided a running commentary on towns, with scenes of animals running along beside the train rails as they spun by. Dora anticipated the trip, because at least she would be with Lou, the family together again. She imagined it day by day with stops in charming rustic towns along the way, an idealized journey.

Dora didn't quite understand exactly how everything would proceed, but for now the light in her children's eyes as their father outlined the trip was enough for her. She was drawn into the magic Lou could weave and, for the moment at least, she didn't focus on the destination.

And so, Lou's dream became reality. Lou, Dora, Jesse, Jack, Sally, Eliza and Mabel Stokes struck out. The train journey captured the children's sense of adventure in ways Dora couldn't have foreseen. The train itself, with mysterious workings, sounds, smells, the shouting of the workmen, all combined to occupy all waking moments. Jack ate and slept, and even as he was held up to the train windows, to observe what the others saw, he turned his head to his mother as the most interesting focus. Jesse threw up his hands at the lack of curiosity of his brother. He instead listened to Lou and received all the education he craved.

In a month, Lou, Sally, Jesse and Eliza were back in Ogden. Dora, Jack and Mabel were quite comfortable at the house in Montana. The place had been made more presentable. Dora had a good store of what she needed with more on the way as she looked forward to Lou's imminent return. All the while thinking that, at least for the present, the children, Jesse and Sally, would start school and Lou would continue to build his business, so dearly put together years before. Then, as he would put others in charge, building on the ground work he had laid, he would remain in Ogden, benefitting from the onsite procurement and future consolidation with not only the Coreys, but newer businesses coming West to reap the rewards of a sure transportation and construction boom.

Dora read his most recent letter:

My dear love, I am still in Ogden. W. W. Corey will be here in the morning I think and then something will be arranged. Your letter written Monday came today. I wish I was with you, or rather you were here, which would be more pleasant for us all. I went with Bill to cut kindling at 75 cents for two sacks. He hired a boy to do most of the work. I don't believe you have met Bill, fine fellow. So far, he has cut about four dollars' worth but mother is willing to pay it. Sally is helping with the dishes and other chores. Her turn is every other day. Jesse doesn't like the kitchen duty but when he's finished, he can read his magazines undisturbed. I bought him a copy of H. G. Wells The First Men in The Moon *and he calls anyone he doesn't like a selenite, whatever that is. Haven't read it myself and then there is his grasp of everything about airships. Do you believe Wilbur Wright flew again for 39 minutes? A little far-fetched but not for our Jesse. Now how is our Banner Boy, little Jack? You know I think he's going to favor me. Will that make you happy? Well love, be patient. I almost felt like I had done you a great injustice in leaving you there, but you have your checkbook and money and I'll send for you very soon. Lovingly, Lou.*

Dora wrote from Straw, Montana:

Dear Lou, I'm leaving for Ogden in the morning. This is the last straw and I don't mean Straw, Montana. I'm glad everyone feels well, I suppose Pike too, not to leave him out and you know I love him. I know the love you send is true. I've never questioned it. Jack is a happy baby but what are we doing up here? I am not going to homestead or anything else in Montana. I've tried understanding. How is the canning going to get done, your mother wrote a few days ago, canning? I can't think of a nice answer. I love you, please let us live together, Pol.

Dora scanned another letter while holding Jack on her hip, jostling him as she paced the small room. She reacted viscerally as she read the phrases, reaching to turn the envelope over as it had landed on its side. It was from Ogden.

Lou wrote, *Dear heart, what can you be thinking?* What indeed. *Have I taken you to Montana with my darling baby and left you there?*

Yes, Lou, that's just what you have done.

I can tell you the awful story in more detail when I see you. I won't try to harass you with details.

Dora thought the details would help. He needed to save the day, details to follow about the business, someone wasn't doing his work and Lou had to step in. He had arranged to borrow $25,000! How on earth could that have happened?

Dora laid Jack, now asleep, on the bed and took the chair by the table, where she spread the sheets flat and moved on down the page.

Dora was worried about Lou's state of mind. He seemed delusional about what was possible in his business. He could not meet any requirements for a loan. He didn't have the cash needed to play in whatever game involved rail construction, let alone dams and canals. He knew the talk and hard work, but beyond that he was out of his depth, and it broke Dora's heart.

He hastened to add that Eliza was better and even Pike the dog and the children were content. Content! He brought the letter to a close hoping that she would be content herself.

Well goodbye and lots of kisses and love for baby and your own good self, Lou.

She wept over Lou, hundreds of miles away from her, continuing to distance himself. She reached for Jack, who was nearly asleep beside her on the bed. His grimace at being awakened was an indictment of her mothering abilities, so stifled of late, and she hugged him fiercely. She with difficulty held back her tears to soothe him as she then lay across the bed to nurse him.

Dora returned to Ogden and received this letter from Winnipeg:

Dearest Polly, how do you like it? Doesn't it seem better than Canada? How would you like to see the snow we're having here? It is rather more sleet than snow but cold as can be. It is much worse than Calgary. I shall be back there in about a week. I hope I shall have letters from you when I return telling me all about Blackfoot. Your Montana letter pleased me very much.

In what way? Dora thought. The Montana adventure was over, and her thinking had moved to a new level. She could no longer afford to be out of contact, let alone out of sight of Lou. She feared for his mental stability, in fact.

A statement such as, *I was glad you were all busy*, had no meaning. Yes, she was busy doing the work she was made for, loving her family, and, aggrieved, longing for Lou, too embarrassed to ask for comfort, when it was her joy and vow to provide it.

At this point Dora surmised that an earlier letter had crossed the latest letter's path somehow.

Be sure that you can put enough by from the rental money and Frank can give you what you need to have the flour and pork barrel and the coal house full. We learn from home that the company was awarded the promontory job. This is a nice piece of work and can be done in the winter time so I guess I have a job as I get home for the balance of the year. Tell me about everybody at home. With love to all, yours, Lou.

In September of 1907, Dora received the last letter from Lou, from Butte. She held the one-page letter in her hand and read and reread it, saying aloud some of the phrases, the letters, as was Lou's custom, strung together as if in one word. *Noone to meetyou.* She said it again . . . *noonetomeetyou,* mesmerized by Lou's thoughts which she knew so well.

I can't get over my last glimpse of you on the platform with baby and noonetomeetyou.

He had begun the letter, *Let me hear from you at Ogden, how you made out.* Not an intimate opening really, even as it followed the salutation, *Dear love.* Then he lapsed, as he often did, into the mundane. *I came here from Livingston this afternoon, too late to catch the four o'clock train and am held up until two forty-five a.m. and will be home Sunday night.*

Did he know how she would ache for his travel rigors and routine, at odd hours, no food, without a clean bed which he would always find at home? And he said he would arrive Sunday. She mouthed the words; I will be home Sunday night.

He had said that he thought she would be all right. How could he possibly believe that? All right as she traveled with Jack, all right as she arrived and sought a way to the house, all right without him again?

I love you dear with all my heart. She broke into racking sobs at that sentence and could only read with difficulty, as she stood in the kitchen. *I was cussed lonesome over in Livingston without my ----- companion.* She couldn't read the word before companion. Was it constant? Surely not that: constant companion denoted being with him all the time, through cold and grief and happy times, she could remember, but not as she remembered him the last time. He was nearly gone from her, she knew he was ill and she was powerless.

$\sim$

Lou was in great discomfort. He feared not only Dora but his mother would see the change in a short time. He could see in the mirror the effects of his poor habits. He lived too long on coffee and cigarettes. The swelling in his feet was painful and he saw that puffiness had crept to his face as well, especially under his eyes. The backache was almost secondary to these more visible symptoms of whatever had caused such a slump in his former state of robust health.

Lou reread Dora's latest note, and then again. As for Dora, Sunday night was too far away. She wrote to Lou:

I want you here now, even Jack but surely Sally and Jesse would be a new little man with his handsome father home . . . and your wife, that's me dear one, whatever has happened? I certainly haven't been your constant companion of late. Come quickly without delay, D.

Nan had left. Bessie gave Lou the message, second hand, from Nan's note. Bessie claimed she had misplaced it, but the gist was that Nan had moved East with Tommy and wished Lou well. All fight in Lou was gone, he had been striving unrealistically to be with Nan, an effort never meant to yield a new life, and the cost? His life with Dora in Ogden.

The letter, which Lou never saw, began: *Dear Lou, I'm taking Tommy back east to get good schooling and be with boys his age. Here he can only get worse. I slapped his face the other night, caught him in a lie about where he had been, I know smoking and for all I know into drink with his rowdy companions. Bessie's family will have me back. They know other families who need a woman like me to run things and tend to their children, that at least I can do. Please don't write to me. I'll have enough of you in my mind as it is. Now I want just that alone, since I can't have the other. My mother would have called my thoughts wild and they are that for sure, but thoughts of you must fade somehow. I will not say what you know I feel only that; I want your happiness. I can't feel kindly to her and know we would be like oil and water should you take me to wife like your pa did, ha. I truly don't sound seemly and forgive me but I'm not ashamed, only sorry I delayed. Something led you to see me and I'm glad for it. Maybe it was the loneliness, but I always think it was more than that. Bless you Lou. Nan.*

◦──

Lou had lost weight and his color was not of a man who was outdoors, pursuing vigorous activity, but that of a man not getting enough sleep and eating less than nutritious food. Lou's arms hung by his sides. Dora's own heartbeat mirrored the pulse she could see in his wrist. Their bodies often matched the position of the other, Dora had observed many times across a room, hands folded or not, one hand on the chin, both hands clasped in a way that was exactly like the other.

Lying side by side in years past, so few years, they matched their very breaths, remarking, fascinated by the wonder of their good fortune, breast to breast, hands knowing the history of each other, pulsation in their throat dissolving into giggles on Dora's part, throaty laughter from Lou. All this before 1898.

Dora stood to touch the chopped off greying hair, bristly compared to the soft golden curls she used to caress. They had known each other since childhood and were now joined as promised in their vows for time and all eternity.

The chopped hair was a matter of fact way of dealing with head lice acquired on his last foray farther north, much of it camping, some nights in hotels where fresh linens did not exist. Dora shuddered to think of this last reality, all to enable him to work for her and the children to better their lives at the expense of his own. She choked back tears and turned away even as she longed to hug him to her breast. Anger warred with tenderness, all past decisions having irrevocably etched the pattern of their lives. The joy of memory floated above them like wisps of smoke.

From October on, Lou's condition slipped daily. Friends came by to see him and shed tears as they left the house and pressed Dora's hand. Eliza returned from St. Louis after a wire from Dora reached her. She said immediately it was Bright's Disease, and every hour confirmed it. The treatments she recommended—enemas and hot baths, which he tolerated for two days then begged off with no resumption planned—would reverse his condition. In her opinion, Lou couldn't be moved safely even if there were a physician in Salt Lake who could intervene in a substantial way. There was blood in Lou's urine, and he was in considerable pain passing even a small amount.

At least he was home with Dora and their children. At first, Sally shied away from him, so altered was his appearance, but Jack stayed close. Lou propped himself in the bed to make a place for him. Jesse shared his treasured science magazines and books and his dreams, too. He said he would be a soldier like his dad. Lou wept at that.

Lou died in his sleep beside Dora in late November.

The memorial service was conducted by the Elks Lodge, his friend John Edward Carver providing the eulogy. His voice was strong, but as he told Dora, his heart ached for his friend. Dora, dressed in a henrietta and moire dark blue dress, sat composed, her children at her side.

Frank Elgin had been a behind the scenes supporter, taking care of details which never came to Dora's attention. He saw that Lou's brother Joe, and Dora's Mound Fort family, had nearby lodgings at his own expense. He and Annie both provided comfort as needed but did not intrude if family were present.

The rector of Good Shepherd Episcopal Church, Albert Brown, came to the service as well as two vestry members who were close friends of Frank and lodge brothers of Lou. Friends from the ward provided food, child minding and many comforts practical and emotional.

In the following days, others came to the house on 28th Street to be of help. One afternoon, as Dora was resting, Annie answered the door to find David O. McKay standing on the porch. He entered, his tall frame accentuating the smallness of the parlor. As Dora entered from the other room, hearing a voice, he took her hands in his own. Dora had known him for many years through her work in the schools. He stayed for just a moment declining refreshment but, as she told others, lifted her spirits immeasurably on a particularly dreary day.

          ◅◹

Frank always made himself available for any need. His sister Annie made sure the children were kept engaged with either Delia or other children in the ward. She herself enjoyed time with Sally, for she needed patience. Jesse had his books and sought future dreams as escape from a life in Ogden, now without the possibility of fatherly companionship. Frank gingerly tried suggesting various activities to foster, if not closeness, at least conversation with Jesse.

He intended to ask Dora to marry him as soon as a period of mourning had passed. He saw no advantage in delaying what he knew could be a good life for her and the children. He only hoped that in time Dora would love him as he loved her.

Chapter Twenty-Nine
Dora at Home

Dora kept Jesse and Sally home from school even beyond the joyless Christmas holiday. Now they were both anxious to see their friends again. She waved as they trudged off. If not for Jack, she would have followed them. Perhaps her friend on the school board, Ida Taft, would place her as a teacher in the fall. She had her teaching certificate, somewhere among her papers. Lou had once told her if she could find it, he would frame the document and hang it proudly. Now it was too late to collect on that good-natured promise.

Pulling her shawl more closely around her shoulders, Dora mused further about a possibility for work. The money would help, and she would not feel so shut in. Delia could watch Jack. He would benefit from having Delia engage him in conversation as he followed her around during her daily routine. Better company than his mother in most respects, Dora thought.

Dora considered taking the streetcar on Saturdays to work at the library, perhaps afternoons to start. Later she might work other days. She could take the children on Saturdays. Sally could look at her books, Jesse work on his lessons, then go to the store to help his uncle Joe. So many possibilities.

But as she closed the side door behind her and looked around the familiar kitchen, she knew her plans were premature. She would see The Broom Hotel on the corner of 25th Street from windows on the north side of the library, and she'd see it whenever she left the building to walk in the park. It would freeze her heart. The three days and nights she and Lou had spent there, after their wedding in Logan, surfaced often with precise detail. The couple had looked out their corner bay window at the young city scene as if it was their kingdom. In their eyes, the city hall rivaled any European castle. Lights below revealed a glittering city of friends and well-wishers. No, the location of the library building would place her in direct view of the hotel.

Since Lou's death, friends, especially Frank, had shopped for her to unburden Delia. Then, more and more she relied on delivery to her home to not take advantage of Frank's kindness. The downtown scene, without Lou's presence, had lost its magic.

Annie had urged her to help in the store, informally, just to get out. Even thinking of a call to Ida now put her in a state, and she put it off. What would she tell her? She certainly couldn't unburden herself to Ida, of her run of fatigue. She could have confided in Eliza, who had once commented that they were of the same cloth, but from different bolts, and there was always a possibility of a mismatch where pattern is important. From Eliza, this was a means of comfort. Something from Eliza's well-worn medical bag was needed, and as Eliza had peered at her, Dora simply needed to speak up, but she didn't. This condition was beyond an iron tonic or a dose of salts.

Jack slept twice a day for an hour. Dora reserved the morning for chores, afraid callers might see that she was not keeping up her home. She brushed and swept, fluffed pillows, oiled furniture, then sat at the table and looked at the brittle lilac bush by the porch. Lou always brought her the first bloom, deep purple with a smell of grapes, along with the small branch it clung to. She placed the stem in a pale green jar on her kitchen window. Now she rested her head on her arms on the table. She was too tired to look at the lilac and didn't care this year if it bloomed or not. Maybe she would have Jesse dig it out of the ground. Of course, it might have the opposite effect and cheer her. She prayed for that, but without much faith.

When Jack awoke, they would have bread and milk and always some fruit—dates or an apple—then bundle up for a walk. Dora craved fresh air even if it was blustery, and Jack didn't mind. His abundant blond curls would be covered by a serviceable wool cap, the one Eliza had knitted for Jesse. His chubby legs wouldn't feel a hint of cold, encased in brown corduroy. Blue nubby mittens were the last coming home surprise from Lou and these almost forgotten in his grip at his return, so preoccupied did he seem, ill and exhausted from his journey.

One afternoon, Dora took up a still usable small winter coat, the collar decorated with wool flowers, which had been cut down from one of Sally's. No neighbor was going to point to Lou's Banner Boy in girl's clothing. More as a distraction than a critical chore, she set about carefully snipping away the yarn strands of rose and gold. My, Lou would have been cross at such an idea! He was firm about some things. He rose to a boil but just as quickly the bluster was gone. Dora would be enveloped in his arms, lifted and whirled about the room. Her breath caught in her throat at the thrill of the uncertainty. Often, he would unceremoniously set her on her feet, further taking her breath away, in fact, with kisses.

These times had been overshadowed of late by his morose, dark moods and puzzling reticence and lack of certainty about future plans. Lou had dodged any talk of weakness.

Now it was clear why he had guarded his physical symptoms. Letters of the last year, and the more frequent separations, even Dora's fear that he had found female companionship in Montana during the long winter just a year ago, caused Dora no little anguish. What was it, then, that had so confirmed his resolve to go back continuously to what he sought, a new start for them, delving in a world without her, and without Jack, Sally and Jesse?

Dora had to, at this point, examine two very different trains of thought, besides the purely medical concerns. Rejected out of hand was the idea that Lou was going to leave her and start a new life with someone else. All that she knew of him and his most recent, as well as past, desire to have her with him, simply fought against that train of thought. How many times had the biblical phrase echoed, not in the same context as in the Bible itself, but the call to "come and see": Lou's wanting to literally have her drop everything to come and see, either what he had made or repaired. She frequently responded with exasperation at leaving some needed task, to scurry to him. She wished now she could go back and respond positively every time he had called.

Lou wanted the family all together, that was clear. The trips were difficult, and her resolve remained to not leave permanently, but whatever the grouping need at the time, the eventual goal was to be together.

Opposing this rosy explanation was the puzzle over Lou's chill around her. Formerly, even when overworked, he had, as a young man, still showed exuberance, teasing her, catching her unawares with lusty embraces and kisses that left her breathless. However, if she enumerated or worse checked her calendar, the truth would be told. From his most recent visits, thankful though she had been to see him with the children, she couldn't honestly say that she didn't care if he reached for her in their bed, or sought to renew the warmth even Jack conveyed who was profuse in his demonstrations of very physical affection. Her scalp tingled at the thought of Lou with any other woman. She shut her eyes tightly to blot out any such image.

⌒

Dora dreaded the appointment with the photographer. At the same time, she was proud of her youngsters and wished to show them at their best, well cared for and healthy. Mr. Lester positioned the four for optimum effect. Jack squirmed only until Dora gave him small bits of hard candy twisted in a handkerchief to suck on. Sally looked bright as a dollar, pleased with a large taffeta hair bow which made up for the fact that she was not allowed to wear her flowered jumper. Jesse looked striking, even at twelve. Somber and fully conscious of his position as eldest male and head of the family, yet somehow, he was unable to comprehend fully what his responsibilities might be. Dora's appearance was serene, her presence ostensibly accepting of her widowed state.

The photographer positioned the four again to enhance the pose. Being a funeral photograph, the subjects were told not to smile. He nodded his approval as he completed the composition.

"There!" The comment was such an exclamation that Dora saw Sally jump, her right knee at the time propped on a stool in back of Jesse for balance. After she was put to right, Sally eyed the whiskered man with some suspicion. She would be ready next time. Oliver Lester scurried noisily from front to back of the camera completing his task. He breathed with a moist in and out swoosh of breath which Dora disliked, but after all, the fee had been less than Ford's, which the family had used in years past. He had been patient with Jack, letting him hold the studio cat after the sitting.

Dora intended to forward one photo to Eliza out of respect for Lou. She had left to visit a friend in the East a week after the funeral. Though Dora hadn't expected any increased emotional support from her, still, living next door, Dora would have thought Eliza might stop in during long evenings. Her mother-in-law's practice had slowed somewhat as more young doctors had moved to Ogden. Still her delivery services, especially in the case of long-established families, were sought, as public records showed.

Eliza had commented that at least Dora had the children, and she had become used to Lou's absences during the last third of their marriage, a union of seventeen years. Her children, lovely as they were, in no means made up for the energetic man she had wed. She gave her mother-in-law the benefit of the doubt. Eliza had lost a son, two grandchildren and a husband in just a few years and didn't always show her feelings, but she was always engaging with Dora's children.

Much to Dora's relief, friends from the ward, after the initial sharing of meals and food, stopped by with less frequency. Alice Darby had understood, having lost her youngest a few months before, but none of Dora's friends had lost their husbands.

A few months after the funeral, John Edward Carver sent Dora a note saying he would like to call. Would she get word to him if that would be convenient?

Dora saw his tall figure striding up the walk at exactly the time noted; she was glad to see him. The late autumn wind whipped a fringe of hair as he removed his hat and unwound a serpentine scarf from around his neck. He stamped loudly on the side porch to clear his feet of dust.

"Dora, my dear," he said, as she opened the door wide. He clasped her hands in his.

"Dr. Carver, please come in. I've been looking forward to your visit." Dora ushered him into the parlor, now used less formally for the children's inside play and study needs. Since it was comfortably warm, thanks to the small gas stove, Dora often sat there interacting and observing her children's activities as she sewed or mended.

All was brushed and tidy. There were fresh doilies on the furniture. A gangly green plant enveloped the lamp table, the lamp's base devoured by stems and leaves. An amber glow washed the walls around Dr. Carver, thrown by the colored glass Lou had installed above the door and in the west-facing window. Unchanged was the table below it, now set for three with a high chair for Jack.

"Dora, please call me John. We've been friends for a long time, and Lou and I had such a strong bond of brotherhood even though I am not of your faith." He settled his tall frame comfortably in the large armchair.

"Of course, John. I'm afraid I don't have tea, would coffee do?"

"Coffee is always welcome on a brisk day. Often when I make calls, tea seems to be more favored, but actually I prefer coffee with just a drop of cream."

"I've made molasses cookies; you know, for the children. They're in the tin on the table." Dora felt somewhat awkward. She rose quickly to fetch some plates from the cupboard and napkins from a drawer. Ordinarily, she would have had all in readiness for the visit. As she had opened the ice box door for the cream, Dora's eye was drawn to the whimsical Jack Frost name plate.

Lou had chosen this ice box over other brands, because Jack Frost was a familiar character from one of Sally's picture books. Sally and even Jesse had set about making competitive drawings of how Jack Frost himself would appear, as winter frosted the tree limbs and he jumped from branch to branch in their imagination.

Dr. Carver's question broke into Dora's reverie and she wondered how long he had been waiting for his cream. "Are the children at home, Dora?"

Dora returned with the cream and took her seat. "Jesse is at Mother Jensen's studying with her." The Mother Jensen term was disingenuous, but Dora bowed to convention when referring to Lou's mother out of respect when in conversation with others. "She thinks it's important for him to be tutored at home in addition to school. I know she would like to send him East for schooling. He's very bright, and I agree."

At school, Jesse applied himself in mathematics, thinking of being a draftsman or even an architect. He was artistic and covered his schoolbook inner covers with the stylized initials, L. J. J. Jealous of slightly older friends who went to more socials, his appetite for them was increased by dancing class attendance, paid for by his grandmother. He liked his best clothes far better than what he wore to school each day. The two women in his life were committed to his being well turned out. Though from what he regarded as a poor family, Jesse's father had been respected by the community, and Jesse stood a little taller when recognized as Lou's eldest son. Whether out of pity or genuine regard, social invitations increased from the prominent families in town. Jesse preferred these activities to being assigned the chore of brushing Pike, his grandmother's dog.

Jesse had little to do with Jack; he didn't know anything being a baby. Sally, being only a girl, was content with her picture books. She thrived on looking endlessly at fabric samples and ribbons, courtesy of Annie. She didn't seem to mind at all having clothes made over from old things of Eliza's. Jesse wanted new things like some of his friends from well to do families. He planned someday to go back East to school, perhaps St. Louis or, better yet, Chicago. He would rub shoulders with fellows who wouldn't dream of wearing anything not bought in the best shops, and they, he assumed, would marvel at his polish, being a Westerner.

"But would you like that, Dora?" Dora then brought in the coffee pot on a small tray, taking a moment to compose herself, judging that her routine must have looked haphazard to Dr. Carver.

Dr. Carver's reassuring smile confirmed what was in her heart, that unless she herself traveled with Jesse and Sally and Jack as well, there would be no more separations in her family, at least in the foreseeable future.

Dora knew that Jesse would welcome a chance to move East. Frank Elgin was his ideal now. In Dora's opinion, Jesse showed the effects of having been separated from his father at critical times in his young life. Sally's head would be turned by new playmates, given her very young perspective, and having new fabrics to turn into her own special design projects. Jack would be only too happy to be entertained by a new array of adults who would think him delightful.

One afternoon Jack had looked up at his brother and asked, "Are you my father?" Since Jesse at twelve was a towering figure to Jack, the question was understandable.

Jesse had turned on his heel and left the room, muttering, "This is the last straw", using a favored family phrase. Dora knew that at fifteen, her son wanted to be on his own, to study and better himself. Dora admitted to herself that being a big brother, let alone a father figure, was not what Jesse wanted.

Again interrupting her chain of inner thoughts, Dr. Carver continued. "Dora, I know that a decision to join Frank would not be an easy one, not yet of course, but he has spoken to me and the rector of Good Shepherd about his love for you."

Dora was struck by the ease of examining such a choice in her parlor. She didn't flinch, didn't wonder. If Lou could look in on her from above would he be appalled at the conversation? Perhaps he would agree that she should seek a happy life for herself and their children.

"Frank's sister Annie is a lovely young woman and, biased though she may be, it would cheer her greatly to have you for a sister. I have been to St. Louis many times and I know that you would find it a welcoming home with so many opportunities for the children." He took Dora's hand in his. "Lou was one of my dearest friends and I know of no moral flaw in him. He thought of all of you as he worked and that is how he did what he did.

His illness perhaps couldn't have been avoided, given the goals he sought and the energy with which he pursued them." He smiled. "I will keep you and your family always in my prayers, Dora."

"Thank you, John, I will take into consideration your counsel. I'm receiving the same from Annie and Eliza, not surprisingly. I agree that Frank is a fine man and would be a conscientious father to my children."

"And a devoted husband to you, Dora. Well, goodbye and call me if you want to talk further."

As Dora watched from the porch, he reached the street and turned to wave. She marveled at her measured conversation with the minister, hoping that her demeanor in no way betrayed her inner turmoil.

"Why can't I leave as others leave me?" Dora said out loud. Dr. Carver, trudging away, had other places to go. He disappeared down the hill as Frank had done. Even Eliza would leave in her brusque way, sturdy brown alligator bag in hand, giving Dora a gentle pat on the back rather than a hug.

Dora easily fell into self-pity of late, ineffective in generating a healthy atmosphere around herself and her remaining family. Delia often took the reins in making decisions relating to Dora's house as well as in Eliza's. Then even Delia traveled more often to visit relatives in the northern farming community of Corrine. They had all left. Even Tillie had died many years before, after the two girlhood friends had pledged to always be close and that their offspring would grow up together. And Lou, who had already left her in every other way, was now gone physically.

Dora sagged as she watched from her window or drooped at the porch railing, nearly sinking to sit on the porch floor. If passersby saw her, no matter. The web of dead vines would mask her presence.

And now Frank had left again, after recently bringing some routine papers for Dora to sign. Afterward, he moved briskly with purpose, no doubt, to care for the persistent needs of his clients. Dora knew he could have signed the documents in her stead. She flattered herself that he'd come solely to see her, but he certainly didn't linger this time. She sensed, for good or ill, that he would have refused an offer for tea, and in truth, it was late in the day and he was clearly on his way home. But he had, Dora mused, walked all the way up the hill to her house and would, on leaving, have over a mile to reach his apartment. Was there hope in her mind, did she dare think that Frank saw her as he apparently had confided to others, as a wife? Why hadn't he said anything, had her previous rebuff stung him too deeply?

Dora's Mound Fort family had retreated from her daily thoughts, even her prayers. It seemed as though Nannie had emerged as her mother's favorite companion, along with Nannie's family, numbering three sons and four daughters. Hugo, the oldest son and right hand of late, and husband Edgar, homebound after a stroke, required most of her needs. Hugo hadn't yet found a future marriage partner after returning from his mission, and Nannie was taking advantage of his availability. Besides, Nannie said, Hugo reminded her to a fault of her husband. Their home, the last time Dora visited, was dour and uninteresting, without the fanciful touches Dora had always sought to provide in her rooms. Beige was the color of the walls throughout, unrelieved by paper of any kind. Curtains were closed to guard the surprisingly bright carpets. The end effect was dimness and, in Dora's mind, showed a need for fresh air and sunshine.

Nannie's once glossy red hair had dimmed. It was confined with the aid of pomade in a rigid unbecoming style. Dora smiled as she recalled Lou's vigorous brushing of her own hair. She couldn't imagine such fun-filled times between Nannie and her husband.

As Dora evaluated many of her own opinions, she judged them to be petty if not unkind. She had last spoken with her sister a few months before and Nannie had voiced her wish to come to Ogden soon for a visit on her own, and the entire exchange put Dora's teeth on edge.

"Now how exactly shall I come?" Nannie's newly acquired whine was nearly visual.

Dora left the sarcasm undisguised but couldn't resist saying, "All the way to 28th Street?"

Dora could not suppress a smile. In fact, if Annie had seen her, she would have been downright critical of Dora's light response to Nannie's quandary.

"I must have Hugo bring me, I wouldn't make the trip alone. I'm still nursing Louise. She is so colicky, you just don't know, Dora, the sleepless nights. But I endure somehow." This was followed by a deep sigh.

As they spoke, Dora's eyes roamed her ceiling. A cobweb caught her attention.

"Are you still there, Dora?" Nannie conveyed unmistakable petulance.

"Yes, yes, dear, I was just thinking. I must go . . . someone's on the porch." Dora saw no one on the porch but she unceremoniously hung up the phone. That afternoon, before Eliza's return, she would have the cobweb swept aside if she had to climb on the dresser to do it.

When Eliza had returned from St. Louis most recently, she had glanced at Dora's parlor drapes which did, on close examination, appear dusty. Eliza blurted out, "What have you been doing, Dora, with your time, dear?"

"Mother Jensen, I simply didn't want to do it. I am in a state of profound grief and, and I think the drapes are just fine." At that, she strode from the room and didn't care what her mother-in-law thought.

Eliza's tone was abrasive; Dora could see none of Lou's nature in her.

⌒

Many nights Dora lay wrapped in one of Lou's flannel gowns. She returned to her memories for comfort, saying his name and hearing him say hers. Fatigue and grief eventually lulled her to sleep. She tumbled and turned, pressing the pillow to her mouth. She cried little in front of the children. She knew they needed to cry themselves and she needed to be there for their comfort and, besides, none of their tears would bring Lou back again.

There had been inevitable household changes. Sally and Jesse slept in the large iron bed where their parents had slept, now with Jack between them. Dora used a daybed in the parlor where Lou's body had been on view for mourners. Just a few months before muffled comments were heard there, from Lionel Herrick and D. K. Maughan, both of whom had written encouraging letters to Lou as they heard of his illness. They in all innocence had expected a full recovery for one of their own, an Ogden man of promise, not of wealth but of moral substance.

One morning Dora was awakened by Sally's entrance, after sliding open the doors which separated her during the night from her children.

"Papa, are you here yet?"

Dora, barely awake, sat up twisting her hair into a loose coil, catching it with sturdy pins. Sally's face fell as she saw only her mother, not the tousled haired figure of her father, his suspenders falling in loops under his arms as he shaved at the bowl, twisting his rubbery face to accommodate the razor. He had often made clown faces for his daughter with a finishing dollop of shave lather on her nose as well as his own. Her name was Jane Ellen, but Lou had decreed it too stuffy. "I always liked Sally for a name." She had always been Sally thereafter, with no argument from Dora.

Dora still nursed Jack first thing in the morning. The stove's gassy smell prompted her to open the window a crack, although it was bitter cold weeks on end the year Lou died.

Jesse pushed back noisily from the table. "Good stoves don't smell."

Dora motioned for him to take his opinion outside.

Saturday mornings the children were led from one activity to another. Going for a walk, Jack bundled in wool, pulled none too willingly by Jesse. Dora pointed out anything of interest: a bird on the path, cloud formations and always watching for the first signs of green, even among the weedy growth in the fields between the houses as they walked south to north on Monroe. They would return, walking up 28th Street on the north side. As they came back down, Dora stopped across from the house. It was modest by some measure, but the home Lou had fashioned for them, one they intended to live in for many years. At times, she wondered if applying all the gingerbread she had wanted had shortened Lou's life, so rigorous had been the stretching and numerous climbs up the ladder. Some of the trim had been applied only a few months before his last trip north.

After they scurried across the street and entered the kitchen, she and the children thawed out and had bread, butter and warm milk with the addition of a small lump of brown sugar dissolved into caramel goodness. Delia came to help, especially if Eliza were traveling.

One morning, as Dora returned from a walk by herself, she found Jack on the floor under Delia's watchful eyes, playing with the Bo Peep toy given to Darling by Lou when she was only two. As she outgrew interest in the toy, it had been placed on a high shelf. Dora caught her breath to see it in Jack's hands.

Scarcely did she realize the meaning as she said the words, "Life does continue. Papa would have wanted it so." She knew this, yet still the numbness persisted.

Dora could almost hear Lou's voice directing the chores be done just so. He was very firm with the children, always making sure they took no shortcuts, whether in school or in tasks around the house. Jesse was punished one day when Lou overheard him muttering, "This isn't West Point, after all." He thought his father had left by the side door, but it had been Delia coming in.

One late afternoon as Jesse studied and Sally cut out flowers for a scrapbook, Dora was struck by the similarity of their dark curls with her own. Very different from Lou's hair and Darling's pale gold curls. This was a visual tie to Jack whose long blond curls would at some point need to be trimmed. When she impulsively hugged him, "Darling," slipped out, not as an endearment, but the name of the six-year-old girl whose glossy hair was like his own. His older sister, whom he never knew. Jack's life would go on, while Darling's was frozen in time. Dora, Eliza, and Delia were the ones who remembered her best.

Sally and Jesse put Jack to bed, employing a hide and seek game making use of his nightshirt sleeves to cover his hands. Sometimes they made a silly hat for him out of his blouse, pulling it over his ears. The result reflected in the looking glass sent him into gales of laughter and brought a smile to Dora. She recalled Lou's inventiveness in bedtime games and making up stories of frontier life.

After dinner, Jesse saw to a small fire. The grate held coals for the night as Dora sat up late staring at the picture

of Lou on the mantel. This small fireplace was in the parlor where she passed long hours before bed. A music box
was placed on a table near her chair. Frank had brought
it to Sally from St. Louis. It played Yankee Doodle Dandy.
Sally would often take the top off and play it endlessly,
slower and slower, until it finally stopped.

Dora worried as she observed Jesse staring with
dreamy eyes into the orange fire glow, possibly finding
solace in future plans and dreams. He roused himself
only if Dora asked a question about school to draw him
out. She liked to read to him as she had to Lou and had
borrowed a copy of Cassel's *Shakespeare*. Jesse shook his
head no. Dora had to admit the choice of material was
not his. He voiced a preference for science or geography
magazines.

Jesse arose slowly from his place on the rug, stretching out the stiffness which plagued his bony frame. If
lessons were done, he dutifully kissed his mother good-
night and slipped in beside Jack, after pressing his pants
carefully and laying them on top of the blue chest. Dora
told him that when he was a year or two older, she would
make over some of Lou's trousers for him. He scowled
at this.

Dora said, "Jesse, we're not paupers, but we have
to watch every penny. Later you can have some ready-
made pants."

Dora had no doubt that her son would attain a better
life than he now endured. She grasped the gold lavalier
which hung around her neck; it was warm from her skin.
She pressed it to her lips, remembering how when Lou

had given it to her many years before, he had called her his dear kiss, a play on words to repeat the name of her favorite lavender sachet, Djerkiss. Their dreams for the future had been bold. As she walked into the kitchen, she took the familiar steps, humming the music for the Varsouvienne, her toe tapping delicately in the darkened room the better to slide with her imaginary partner. She could feel Lou's hand on her back, the other one gently holding her right hand as they had moved around the floor. She raised her left hand to his imaginary shoulder at the exact height and extended her right hand as she had so many times before. After the dance, Lou would whisper dearkiss in her ear, she could almost feel his breath on her neck as he said it.

In the other room her children noisily readjusted in the bed. Jack was like a warm puppy between the other two. Pete wasn't allowed in the bed but slept contentedly on a clean rag rug by the stove. Dora's eyes fell on the blue chest, somewhat the worse for wear. Forty years before it had held all Eliza's clothes and belongings as she traveled as a new wife from St. Louis, pregnant with Lou. Now it held remnants of the couple's life, school papers of Darling's, Lou's West Point uniform, his gold watch, a pair of shoes Lou had bought for Dora, worn only once to a party, now wrapped in tissue, and dreams, many, many dreams.

Jesse thought it plain, and it was. He had told his mother that he intended to have a fine carved chest when he was a man, to hold his things.

Chapter Thirty
Frank

"I've done everything I can to help since Lou died, everything but . . ."

Dora held up her hand. She knew what he meant. She thought of a sharp retort but it would have been a very dishonest one, so instead she turned physically from Frank and faced the window. She couldn't meet his eyes. Looking out at the view of Ben Lomond, the hot tears came.

"Frank, I need to think about what you have said, offered. I'm acutely aware of all you have done for me in Lou's absence. I know you were his closest friend, but it's just like this . . ."

"If you were aware only of that, and that alone, then Dora, you weren't paying attention."

Frank let himself out of the side door. As he came into view at the front of the house, Dora forced herself to watch him go. He walked west down 28th Street, crossed to the north corner then continued down the hill toward town and was quickly out of sight.

Dora turned back to the room. She loathed it, as it represented the price Lou had paid to provide it. It was as dark as late autumn, with its terrible memory of last year. She almost gasped as she imagined those first signs of spring, the lilacs still tight in bud but inexorably poised to bloom. Never would their fragrance cheer her as they had before, since Lou had planted them by her kitchen door.

Dora remembered the vigor and good sense of Tillie, adept not only with a curling iron, but advice and support. She needed her now to confide in. Nannie would not condone her growing attraction to Frank and would be shocked that, not only was Dora admitting she was in love with Frank, but he was urging her to marry him and move to St. Louis. Tillie would cheer. In fact, she would be focused on matching Dora's earbobs to the bronze taffeta dress she had chosen. In her opinion, Dora could go with a light step and a grateful heart to be his wife.

"Rubbish!" The word would be spat out by Annie as she tried to buoy up her friend's spirits, but more, convince her of the promise of life to come and the care she owed to Jesse, Sally and Jack. The "rubbish" only an expletive to emphasize the idea that it would be ridiculous for Dora to consider *not* accepting Frank's offer.

Frank's proposal so soon after Lou's death was only right, and Eliza approved. Frank indeed had asked her permission to marry her son's widow. To her credit, Eliza thought of the children and, since she traveled as often as she wished, estimated that the St. Louis family would have her as a visitor once a year, perhaps more.

But fact of the matter was that Dora hadn't heard from Frank for nearly three weeks, the longest period since Lou's death, without his thoughtful calling, or arrival of, if not Frank himself, at least a dashed off note, hand delivered by one of the office's messenger boys.

She willed his stocky form to appear at the top of the hill walking toward her house. She had called Annie earlier in the week and thought she detected a slight chill, at least a lack of attention, as twice Annie excused herself to answer requests from her assistants.

Dora had no definite reason to call. She hoped for news of Frank in an offhand way, without having to ask. Dora wanted to hear Annie's welcome voice, even to relay some gossip about which prominent matron just scurried by the shop in a less than fashionably trimmed hat, surely not one of Annie's design. An invitation usually followed from Annie to come down for coffee and pie at Blocks, not to keep Annie too long from the shop. But nothing of the kind was offered. What had Frank said to his sister, that he was at his wits' end over Dora's hesitation, after all it was 1907 and Frank wasn't asking Dora to do anything even remotely scandalous?

It was Frank she wanted to see. The ticking clock mocked her as she looked out the front window. She had no business to discuss. She planned to call him as if there had not been time in between, as if their last parting hadn't been as it was, etched in her memory. The forlorn, last goodbye must be overcome by his exuberant return. Could she possibly convey to him that the emptiness had overcome her? A man so unlike Lou, now an altogether familiar presence, welcomed, even anticipated with, dare she think it, a spirit of giddiness? She wanted to feel his arms around her, to have him pick her up as easily as Sally would be, and he would revel in this ability, the strength of a man holding, carrying his beloved, not as conqueror but lover to be.

Dora's hand was firm as she held the telephone, her voice was quiet but assured as she spoke with Frank and invited him for tea the next afternoon.

The undeniable flutter in Dora's breast as Frank approached the next afternoon, confirmed her decision. He removed his hat and smiled, even before he reached the walkway to the porch. His step quickened, the sun favoring him with a ray of confirming russet glow. And then he was inside the often-used side door and she was enveloped in his husky goodness.

"I'm so glad to see you, Frank." Tears unchecked gathered and a dab of her handkerchief was ineffectual as she took a backward step. Frank's warm gaze betrayed all he felt for Dora.

Her acquiescent smile, her small lovely face framed in the unruly ringlets he adored, left no doubt as to the reality both could now enjoy. A friend of Frank's labeled Dora "the coy widow," of course a friend no more. His Dora! The friend now considered a hateful, jealous individual. Dora was his alone, not by conquest, but by her own breathless admission.

Now forty-five minutes later, conversation had slowed, as they enjoyed the delectable tea Dora had prepared.

Proper small talk had been mixed with references peculiar to Dora and Frank's acquired knowledge of each other and of their life in Ogden.

Barely glancing his way, Dora reached out for his cup and saucer. "Can I get you more tea, dear?" Her raised eyebrows, even as the cup and saucer were lifted, tore through Frank's chest, as he realized that she had no idea of the verbal slip.

He nodded, not trusting his voice. At forty-eight, he was overcome with joy and desire in equal measure. Frank dabbed at his mustache with the snowy napkin and forced himself to remain in the chair. He tried to gauge how quickly he could drink the scalding tea, deciding to ask for an unaccustomed extra measure of cream to cool it so that he could bolt from the house as soon as possible. He must fight the desire to run down the street toward town with his hat in his hand, jubilant for all passersby to see.

Dora glided back to the table placing the cup and saucer in front of him. He thanked her with a smile.

Later, as Frank prepared to leave, he noticed a small glass bottle on the kitchen shelf. He picked it up, a bottle of Djerkiss Sachet. As Dora reached for his hat, she heard Frank say softly, "Djerkiss." He turned the bottle over in his hand. The lavender scent was familiar to him. Dora always wore it.

He looked at Dora in a quizzical way as she seemed to freeze. Then she looked at him as he repeated the now charged word, *Djerkiss,* his voice lower.

Dora reached in back for the counter edge to steady herself. Frank stepped forward, fearing she might faint. Dora turned her head slowly side to side, but then looked at him boldly, remembering Lou saying, "Djerkiss" as he kissed the back of her neck. She wondered how it would feel to be kissed by a man with a mustache, not just any man, but Frank Elgin.

The afternoon had gone from a hearty hello, glad to see you, Frank, to the point where they were both altered by the closeness in Dora's kitchen; intimate space that it was, the unmistakable scent of lavender, the drawing together movement accelerating beyond what they had prepared for. Dora didn't pull away, fixing her gaze on him, mirroring his own . . . he folded her in his arms.

But then their disengagement was clumsy, a mix of mumbled, "I must go," and "The children will be here for their meal." Frank stepped from the kitchen to the door and onto the porch. With a smile and a wave, he was on the front path. Dora turned quickly, her heartbeat in her ears, to watch him go as he had gone so many times; but this was not the same.

Frank chose the most direct route to his home, hardly daring to think, but powerless not to think over each precious moment with Dora, from the first "Hello, Frank." How could anyone else possibly say those words the same way and have the effect they had on Frank? He took the blocks as they sped toward him, first west down the hill with ease. Before he knew it, he was on the street to take him north to his home on the west side of the park.

He took the steps two at a time, having withdrawn the key from his pocket a block away; and he was inside, coat tossed toward a chair. He poured water from a carafe at his desk, gulped a glassful, and loosened his tie as he sat down in his desk chair. He reached for his pen.

Dear Dora, I love you and want you to be my wife. Please consider this a heartfelt and true declaration of my regard for the woman you are and my commitment in our future to your welfare and that of Jesse, Sally, and little Jack. If in any way I am not what you envision as a partner, then perhaps I've deceived only myself, never you.

With fervent hope, Frank.

He fought the desire to hand deliver it, but in the end his impatience gave way to propriety. The note went by regular post, arriving with the Saturday morning mail.

As Dora read the letter from Frank, she noticed that only his signature was decorative. The body of the letter was in a mixture of half printing and the rest cursive, as she was used to on the numerous papers she had had occasion to look at over the years. No, she had never seen his name dashed off with such fluidity and style. She folded the letter, the words still before her eyes; they sang with his now familiar voice, and she imagined him writing it in some haste.

Dora's note came to Frank the next day. His hands trembled as he read it.

Dear Frank, I don't know what to say except, yes Frank, yes! I will come to St. Louis and bring my children. I will marry you and be a good wife, if that will make you happy. I don't know why you have been so good to us but believe you saw good in Lou and knew something worthwhile should come of it. I hope and wish with all my heart that we shall have a happy life together. Your Dora.

Chapter Thirty-One
Memories Put to Rest

Dora worked on a memory book with Sally. She had decided to include things which her children might treasure. Dora had planned to leave it with Eliza, boxing anything too bulky for a scrapbook. Foremost would be a pair of hand-painted shoes brought back for her from Marshall Fields in Chicago. At Lou's direction, they were to complement a pale peach dress worn to a summer dance. She wore them only once, but she couldn't part with them.

Many of Darling's school papers were included, her dancing shoes and a pair of small wooden barbells used in her health exercises. Also, the vividly painted Little Bo Peep toy last played with by Jack. All would be contained in the blue chest, Lou's papers, his black currency box, and all the letters exchanged between Lou and Dora from 1882 until just a few weeks before his death. They were placed in the soft, tan leather purse, a veteran of unwilling journeys north as well as routine errands of a wife and mother; the handle, a reliable teething device for her young children. Dora found her letters to Lou in his saddle bag, carefully wrapped in tissue paper. She found them when, with difficulty, she forced herself to go through every one of his pockets before giving Lou's things away. In addition, in a decorative hat box under her bed, were the children's hair samples, identified and tagged with appropriate pink or blue satin ribbon. In a separate small box lay their hair brushes. Dora wrote out some anecdotal family history documenting how her mother-in-law and her parents had traveled West. Now all except Eliza rested in the Ogden cemetery, L.J. Jensen Sr., Eliza's husband, and now Lou as well, not far from his infant son and six-year-old Darling.

How would Dora remember Eliza? As she saw dimly Eliza's photo across the room, she could appreciate the older woman's history. She had understood being left alone, not only physically but emotionally. How did she deal with the demands of caring for her children with little help at first, and carry on a busy practice? With all Eliza's skill, she had been unable to save those she loved.

When Dora told her about Frank, Eliza prayed, and she was not given to supplication to propel events. In addition, Eliza revealed more of her perspectives on child rearing. "Listen to this, Dora," she adjusted her new glasses, and to emphasize the next thought, she looked pointedly at Dora and held up an article from a journal which she was reading at the time. "Women's place is in the home." Eliza nodded her head for emphasis. "But, Dora, there is a huge need for women to have help with child rearing, for children don't learn just at home but in the community, the library and the public school."

Dora was a bit surprised at some of these ideas, but Eliza did travel widely and maybe women elsewhere had these thoughts.

". . . Our nation's schools must be brought up to an excellent standard." Eliza waved the journal for emphasis. "The family is bigger than what is in an individual home!" She gestured broadly indicating Dora's living room, as it was, a place where Dora thought a rather wide range of learning and creativity was presented for her children at her dining room table.

Dora gave a tepid nod of approval but beyond that didn't trust herself to comment. She found it outrageous to ignore the wholesome bosom of the ward membership, her dear friends, who never tired of educating theirs and others' children. In Dora's mind these ideas were from women elsewhere. She recalled just the week before mailing letters for Eliza addressed to the Utah State Federation of Women's Clubs as well as the National Congress of Mothers. This might explain some of Eliza's thinking.

Chapter Thirty-Two
Crossing the Plains

Dora, wearing a Melrose blue traveling suit, boarded a train with her children and Annie. Lou's brother Joe and his wife Cora, John Edward Carver, Eliza and Delia, formed the farewell party on the platform. They all, each in their own way, had seen the wisdom of Dora's decision. Even Joe, who was taking a more active part in the running of the office, saw the inevitability of Dora's choice. His wife Cora made it clear to her husband that, in her opinion, Dora should remain in Ogden to rear her children; still, she couldn't help admiring the handsome hat which Annie had fashioned to complement Dora's traveling ensemble.

The beginning of the new century saw Sally and Jesse excited about the trip. Jack, no longer called "the Banner Boy", stood on his own feet, happy not to be carried, though his hand was held firmly by Annie.

In a few days, their faces would brighten as Frank's figure appeared on the St. Louis platform. For Dora, it was to be a new life, one with uncertainties and challenges as well as joys. Dora's first time crossing the plains would lead to a much different life than that of her mother-in-law. As the train began to move, Dora looked one last time at Eliza's face; a "thank you" caught in her throat as she waved goodbye.

As it turned out Eliza was already making plans for her next trip East for the wedding in just three weeks. She and Dora were to grow closer than they ever had been. Eliza intended to keep an eye on her grandchildren, not letting them forget they were of genuine pioneer stock.

Notes

1. Djer-kiss: a lavender sachet which didn't come on the market until 1910. I had to include this magical name if only briefly in the story. Dora, my grandmother, always wore this scent.

2. Dora's well-worn purse was a rich caramel color when it was new. Purchased at Z.C.M.I. the year my grandmother was married. It held all the necessities of a woman of that time. The well-worn purse now holds the original letters exchanged between Lou and Dora.

3. The blue chest contained all of my great-grand-mother's possessions as she traveled to Utah with a handcart company in 1868. The chest contains many of the items described in the story.

4. The real Dora died in 1955. She outlived all her children except one, my father, "Jack," in the story. Her house on 28th Street still stands.

5. Eliza in the story was my great-grandmother. Her character, actions, and conversations are partially fic-tionalized though there is much truth there. She did

travel west with a handcart company. She walked a good part of the distance. She was a young wife, pregnant with my grandfather, Lou. He was born in Salt Lake City in 1868. Allowed to help with the delivery of several babies on the trek west, my great-grandmother was influenced to make that her life's work. She was a well-known mid-wife in Ogden where her name is prominent in the Weber county record books.

6. Nan's letter: somewhere lost in the dust of the years, the letter lay in the back of a drawer. Bessie thought it better not to give it to Lou and simply put it in her apron pocket. It was then tossed into a drawer where it worked its way to the back. It was left there as Bessie quit the boarding house in 1909 when she married a drummer and moved to Omaha. After all, she was confident that she had done right by the couple and she did tell Lou most of what the note contained. Given Lou's brief life after leaving Montana, it may have been fortunate that the letter never passed into Dora's hands.

7. In 1898 thirty-two cases of scarlet fever were reported in Ogden, Utah. There were six deaths. Two of these were the infant son and six-year-old daughter of Lou and Dora.

8. Z.C.M.I.: founded by Latter-day Saint leader Brigham Young, Zion's Co-operative Mercantile Institution was one of the first real department stores in the country. In 1868, to counteract non-Mormon business and assure no discrimination by them targeting Mormons with unfair prices, smaller commercial units banded together to form this new entity. At present

the historical façade, familiar to many, with the iconic Z.C.M.I. visible, fronts the present-day Macys in Salt Lake.

9. David Kay: a prominent Ogden merchant dealing in wholesale groceries, and a large range of household necessities. Lou, my grandfather, Louis Jensen Holther Jr. (b. 1868, d. 1907) did work for him and my father, David Kay Holther (b. 1906, d. 1978) was named for him.

10. Relief Society: founded in 1842, even before the Latter-day Saints reached the Utah Territory; concerned with social betterment and education of the women of the church membership.

Acknowledgements

First of all, thank you to Wido Publishing in Salt Lake, the E. L. Marker division, for agreeing to publish *Dear Kiss*.

Initially, I worked with editor Summer Ross, as she guided me through the process, editing at a distance. Over many months, my manuscript underwent changes and some reconfigurations to ready it for further scrutiny. This ultimately led to accepting some new constraints, resulting in a more consistent story line without losing the main strengths I felt my characters exhibited.

My family has continued to be involved in bringing the story I loved to completion. Their reading of sections with critical care provided objective backup as they became more interested in seeing how it would all turn out.

Friends in Ogden, some of whom I had known since grade school, backed the project; especially the ones who remembered the Old Broom Hotel and a popular eatery after which I modeled Blocks lunch room, where several important scenes take place.

In my commitment to authenticity as well as accuracy, though this is a work of fiction, I have read widely and questioned keepers of historical collections. Heather Huyck, friend and historian, author of *Doing Women's History in Public*, gave a critical read to the entire manuscript as well as draft segments. This time was a gift, as she was also working on her own book. Additional support and resource came from Sarah Singh at Weber State University where she heads the special collection area. More informal requests were answered by Linda Harden at Good Shepherd Episcopal church in Ogden as she provided some needed information concerning previous rectors. More than one call was made to Dan Davis at Utah State University who answered my questions about not only what might have been but, in some cases, which of my imagining might have been plausible during the late 1800s.

During the last year, I have been working with WiDo publisher, Karen Gowen, author and editor. With her oversight, still closer editing has been done as well as rooting out inconsistencies and clarifying cultural issues. Her encouragement, as we found points of contact and agreement, made an enormous difference in my resolve to complete the process. I further wish to thank Marny K. Parkin and Steven Novak for the cover art and overall book design.

To my children and grandchildren, who will inherit the letters I found in my grandmother's purse, I say the story is true in spirit if not in every fact, and it honors our family.

To Grant, my companion on this journey of nearly sixty years, for having listened the longest and subdued all things mechanical in my drive to a goal I thought more than once was unattainable, my thanks and love.

About the Author

MARGARET BAGLEY IS A UTAH NATIVE, born in Ogden in 1939. She attended Ogden schools, graduated from the University of Utah, majoring in sociology and psychology. She worked as a special education teacher and has also been employed in healthcare and counseling. She lives near Washington, D.C. She and her husband Grant are the parents of three, grandparents of six. This is her first novel.